PEOPLE YOU'D TRUST
YOUR LIFE TO

BOOKS BY BRONWEN WALLACE

Poetry
Bread and Chocolate/Marrying into the Family
(with Mary di Michele)   1980
Signs of the Former Tenant   1983
Common Magic   1985
The Stubborn Particulars of Grace   1987

Fiction
People You'd Trust Your Life To   1990

PEOPLE YOU'D TRUST YOUR LIFE TO

stories by

Bronwen Wallace

M&S

CANADIAN CATALOGUING IN PUBLICATION DATA

Wallace, Bronwen
People you'd trust your life to

ISBN 0-7710-8791-8

I. Title.

PS8595.A565P46 1990   C813'.54   C90-093091-8
PR9199.3.W355P46 1990

The publisher makes grateful acknowledgement to the Ontario
Arts Council for their financial assistance.

Printed and bound in Canada

McClelland & Stewart Inc.
The Canadian Publishers
481 University Avenue
Toronto, Ontario M5G 2E9

for Jeremy Baxter and Chris Whynot

"Anger and tenderness: my selves.
And now I can believe they breathe in me
as angels, not polarities."
— Adrienne Rich, "Integrity"
A Wild Patience Has Taken Me This Far

CONTENTS

HEART OF MY HEART

There's a story in the paper tonight about this couple who've just married, in their sixties, after forty-five years of star-crossed love. STAR-CROSSED LOVE is how the paper has it, of course, in the caption under the photo which shows them (her grey and plump, him almost completely bald) surrounded by the children and grandchildren from their other (ill-starred, I suppose we could say) marriages. At first glance you'd think it was a wedding *anniversary* photo.

The accompanying article tells how Ned Wilson met Edith Allan, in a London pub, shortly before he was sent to the front.

"Love at first sight," he says. "I knew then and there she was the girl for me. I promised I'd be back for her as soon as we'd put Hitler in his place and I was, too."

Only to find the street where she'd lived in rubble. Neighbours told him Edith Allan had been killed and how was he to know there were *two* Edith Allan's on the same block? So what could Ned do but come home, marry a Canadian girl and raise a family?

"Though I never forgot Edie," he tells us, "Margaret was a good wife and I loved her, but Edie was my heart's core."

"Heart's core." I like that, even as I sympathize a bit with poor Margaret.

And what was Edith Allan (the other, alive Edith Allan) to do, but marry another soldier (Wilf Clarke) and come over with him to Winnipeg where she never ever forgot Ned?

"I knew there was a reason, somehow," she says, "I knew he was no liar. I knew there was an explanation."

And she was determined to have it, it seems; she never let it go. Not for Wilf, not for five babies, not for the death of her youngest sixteen years ago, by drowning, not for the whole forty-two years of their marriage.

"I thought of him every day. I *knew* I'd see him again, one place or the other. But I wouldn't hurt Wilf. So when he passed away last August, I knew it was meant. I knew it was all right to go ahead."

She advertised for him, for Ned, in every paper in Canada.

"Cost me hundreds, but I found him. And he's worth every penny."

Margaret was also conveniently dead when this happened. Frankly, I'm glad. Surely she knew, all those years. Not in words, mind you, but *knew*, by a look, by a hesitation, that though her Ned loved her (and I believe he did, I believe he was good to her) she was not his "heart's core." I think it killed her finally. But gently. I think it wore her out, just as Wilf gave way to the knowledge that what his Edith longed for, held out for, he didn't have.

Sad, yes, terribly sad for those two. But Wilf and Margaret are dead now. Edith and Ned smile. Their children smile. Their grandchildren smile. Why begrudge them a few years' happiness?

I'm always a sucker for stories like this, though the bait this time was the fact that the whole thing happened because there were *two* Edith Allans. In my mind it makes the whole thing *more* intentional as if it really were *meant* to happen.

And I see it this way, of course, because of Mike, the man I think I'm falling in love with for the first time since my divorce five years ago. My friend Marion introduced us at a party in November, but other than saying that he seemed nice and that he was "available," she didn't tell me much about him. We'd seen each other several times before he told me that his wife had been killed in a car accident three years ago. They'd been watching a late movie and during the commercial she'd gone out to Mac's Milk for some chips and dip and a drunk had come through a red light at fifty miles an hour. Only six blocks away, but he hadn't known a thing until they called him from the hospital.

"And even then I thought it was her just phoning to say she'd gone for a pizza instead and did I want pepperoni. I'd already worked it out like that, why she was taking so long. I was so convinced that they had to say 'hospital' over and over before I even heard it."

We were standing in my kitchen making dinner. A late adult meal since the girls were at their dad's that weekend. Mike had been rummaging around for things to put in the salad and I'd suggested artichoke hearts. I'd picked some up specially the day before, like the candles and the wine, planning this scene.

"Great," he'd said. "My wife hated artichoke hearts. I haven't had them in years."

And then it had all come out in a rush. I had the jar of artichoke hearts in my hand, my fingers cramped around it. I didn't see how I could hand it to him or put it on the counter or turn the burner down under the rice.

"What was her name?" It was all I could think of. She was there, in the room, after all. I couldn't just say, "Oh Mike, I'm so sorry," and let her go. No.

"Katherine." Let go, like letting his breath out after stopping the hiccups.

And me, slowly registering that this was an answer, not an appeal, since my name is Katherine, too, the word reaching me so slowly that it seemed much, much later when I finally asked, "Is that what it is for you, then, my name?"

"I'd be lying if I said it wasn't, at least at first. And it's still there, but different. That's why I can tell you now, because I've changed."

He stopped then. Not out of awkwardness, but because there was nothing more to say. I think I was glad he didn't say "Do you believe me?" or "I love you." I like to think that's when I realized I could love him, but what happened at the time was that we just stood there, not even touching each other, until he reached over, took the jar of artichokes out of my hand and turned towards the sink to open it.

Mike lives in Toronto and so far, he's always visited here, I've never gone there. But I'm spending this weekend at his place. I'm dropping the girls off at their dad's on the way out in the morning. They didn't want to go tonight. They're glued to the TV for an hour-long interview with Michael J. Fox.

Sylvia is fourteen, Joanne's nine. From everything I can see they're perfectly content with this constant back and forth between two households. David remarried two years ago and the girls talk to me about his new wife – Carla – as casually as they'd talk about a babysitter or a teacher. She's expecting a baby in March and they're hoping for a brother. They've already asked me what David and I would have called them if they'd been boys. I wonder what they say to David about Mike.

They seem concerned for me, somehow, as if they think I need help. Earlier tonight, when I came down in my pajamas, Sylvia looked up and said, "I hope you're not wearing those old things at Mike's this weekend." More like a college roommate than a daughter. And of course I feel guilty, as if the fact that she can say that takes away from my being a good mother, at the same time that I admire her for it. For being on to me, you might say, for knowing that the difference between our ages alters with the situation. Like the way I'm sitting here now, waiting for her TV show to finish so I can get her to help me decide what to pack.

Below the article about Ned and Edith is a piece about another couple a few blocks from here who've managed to have the name of their street changed from Morris to

Presley, after Elvis. It took them a couple of years to get
their neighbours to sign petitions and to show up with
them at council meetings, but they did it and they think
it was worth the trouble. Their house itself is called
Graceland and the living room is a miniature replica of
Elvis's, stuffed with Elvis memorabilia.

The picture shows them wearing I'VE BEEN TO
GRACELAND T-shirts. I half expect the woman to be Linda
Carlson, the girl who was my best friend in Grade Ten,
but, of course, it's not. This woman has the same fluffy
blonde hair, though, the same dark eye makeup that
Linda – that I also – wore. Only she's still wearing it all
these years later. It's sort of like seeing some part of
myself I'd always thought of as *younger*, with wrinkles
around her eyes and her skin not quite so glowing, and
realizing that she's really kept pace with me all along.

Linda Carlson was a Serious Elvis Fan, whereas I,
though I loved him, was not. I kept getting distracted by
people like Fabian and the Everly Brothers, a lack of
dedication that Linda refused to tolerate. She'd talk
louder than ever when their songs were on the radio, but
if I did that during an Elvis song, she wouldn't speak to
me for days.

She knew the words to every song he ever came out
with. Her absolute favourite was "Don't Be Cruel."
According to what she'd read in *Teen Tips,* it was Elvis's
favourite, too. He had recorded it on July 2, 1956 during
his first session at RCA Victor in New York. He didn't
even know about it when he walked into the studio. He
was just going to do "Hound Dog" and "Any Way You
Want Me" and he didn't even want to do "Hound Dog."
He didn't like it that much, but the guy at RCA said it

would sell. Then, during a break, they happened to play a demo of "Don't Be Cruel," and Elvis stopped everything right there and then and in a few minutes was ready to cut it.

"Don't Be Cruel" was his all-time best-selling record, and Linda believed there was a message in it just for her.

"There, can you hear it?" Linda lifted the needle off and turned to where I was sitting on her bed. "He says my name. I know he's talking to me."

"Linda, he's not saying your name! Don't be such a jerk. How could he even know you exist?"

"Oh, I should have known not to waste it on you! He's saying *Linda. Linda!* Oh, I could die!"

She put the record on again and stood there, swaying, her mouth half-open. A thin stream of saliva gathered and strung from her lower lip. Her eyes slid back in her head. It made me sick. Scared, too. But there was also, of course, something wonderful about it, something attractive.

For as long as I knew her, Linda went on insisting that "Don't Be Cruel" was written for her. It seemed that she would believe it forever. She told me that she played it one hundred times a day and I believed her, believe it still. One Saturday when a bunch of us were downtown together, she spent her entire month's allowance – fifteen dollars – on extra copies of it. I remember us all just standing there in the record store while the clerk pulled the whole stack off the shelf and handed it to her. She kissed every copy before she let him wrap them up. After that we stopped teasing her. It was as if we recognized something delicate, like a stutter or a limp, that we should respect or at least pretend to ignore. And in a way, it *was* like those other physical afflictions; it had the same kind of power over us.

In Grade Eleven, Linda's family moved to Toronto. She wrote for a while, but by the time I started university, we'd lost touch. Sometime later I moved to Toronto for a few months myself. I'd trained as a physio and was doing my internship at Sick Kids, but this day I was just walking along Bloor, near Brunswick, when I heard someone calling me.

It was Linda, though at first I hardly recognized her. She looked smaller somehow, but I put that down to the fact that she was thinner and had her hair cut very short. And she seemed really glad to see me, almost too glad, every gesture exaggerated, the way she threw her arms around me and insisted I come back to her place for coffee.

She lived on the top floor of a large brick house on Sullivan. A beautiful place, full of light, with bright posters on high white walls and plants in the windows and bright cushions thrown casually around. It was the kind of place I wanted to get as soon as I had a job. There was a feeling about it that I recognized then – and still feel now sometimes – as having to do with a woman's really liking it a lot, this living alone.

At least that's what I thought until I reached the kitchen. The smell hit me first, then the heat. It took over everything, surrounded me, like when you step out of an air-conditioned store into a city street in the middle of July. And Linda had stopped talking, too, abruptly, as if she were as surprised as I was. I could feel her silence hanging onto me, like the heat and the smell. A cat-litter box was spilled over near the stove. There were lumps of cat shit everywhere and winding through them, from the fridge to the door, were a row of saucers and bowls, every one caked with cat food, some of it already green with mould. All the windows and the little door that led to the balcony had been taped shut with masking tape. And every wall, from floor to ceiling, was entirely covered with badly xeroxed copies of what appeared to be a newspaper photograph. A darkish man, bearded, wearing a suit, receiving some kind of plaque.

"I was trying to gas myself," Linda said, suddenly. The sound of her voice startled me, I hardly recognized it. "But I couldn't get it to work. I was heading for the subway when I met you. I thought I could jump." The way she said it, she could have been talking about someone she barely knew. "I tried cutting my wrists, too," she went on, "with my Swiss army knife."

She undid the sleeves of her shirt and held out her wrists. They were covered with Band-Aids that had been stuck on any old way, dirty and puckered, so that beneath them I could see the masses of crude, ineffectual cuts and scabs. Some of these were red, crusted with yellow pus. Even the way she held her arms made it seem like they didn't belong to her. All I could think of were those sessions at the hospital, where the surgeons would bring in children with massive burns or fractures, worse than anything I'd seen before, and we'd talk about them in that precise, dispassionate way that made you feel as if the kids had hurt themselves on purpose, so that you could learn new physio techniques. I felt as if I had to measure up to the situation, I guess that's how I'd put it, though I wasn't really sure what that meant. But it seemed important to be casual, matter-of-fact. "How about some coffee?" I said.

At first Linda looked at me sort of stunned, like someone peering in from a long way off. And then her face almost, well, *relaxed* for a minute, as if she finally recognized me. She pushed a chair aside, crawled under the table and sat there against the wall, knees hugged tight to her chest. "You don't need to say anything. Just stay."

I got the window open, put the kettle on and sat down at the table. On it, next to the salt and pepper, were three prescription bottles from three different doctors. Each contained about a dozen Valium.

"If you want to kill yourself," I said calmly, "why don't you just take this Valium with a bottle of wine?"

"Do you think there's enough there? I wasn't sure."

"Absolutely," I said, though I wasn't sure either.

The guy on the wall was a prof in the Biology Department at U of T where Linda worked as a secretary. They'd been sleeping together since she started working there three years ago. She believed he was totally responsible for the fact that she was now intelligent, articulate, beautiful and able to live alone. Before that, I gathered, there'd been a string of boyfriends, none of them very good for her. I could also see that she believed that this guy was. The more she talked, the more she sounded like the old Linda, talking about Elvis. I remember telling myself not to contradict her. That's what I'd learned from before. It was all I had to go on.

Two weeks ago he'd told her it was over. His wife was suspicious and she came first, he'd never said he would leave her, he loved his kids. This was true, he had never said he would and his wife really was nice – Linda had met her. But last night, when she knew they'd gone away for the weekend, she went over to their house, broke in, and with her sewing scissors, which she had brought with her for this purpose, cut every piece of his wife's clothing to shreds. Everything. Dresses, sweaters, underwear, scarves. Even the stuff in green plastic bags at the back of the closet labelled "Goodwill" or "Winter." The lot.

"He'll know it was me. He will, I know he will. And I know he'll call the cops. I've either got to kill myself or get out."

"Where would you go?"

"Well, I thought of that, actually. I could go to L.A. My sister's there. The guy she's with thinks he's going to be a rock star or something."

"How much money have you got?"

"Oh, I don't know, four or five hundred maybe. Enough for a ticket. But there's all my stuff, there's the cat . . . "

"Linda, you were going to kill yourself anyway. What difference does it make?"

(Of course, it seems crazy now, the two of us in her filthy, stinking kitchen, me at the table, Linda under it, talking about whether she would commit suicide or move to California. We drank coffee and smoked Export "A" Plain. I went down to the corner store for the cigarettes after making her promise she'd let me back in. Crazy to think she would, though she did. Crazy to think I could handle it; if she wanted to commit suicide I'd help her. At the time, though, it seemed perfectly normal and I felt in charge. I suppose that's how I got through it, as I got through so much that happened then. All that stuff I refer to when I say "those days are over," thinking I can mean by that that I'm finished with them.)

There was a cancellation on a flight to L.A. for the next morning. Linda's sister was home when she called and said, "Sure. Far out, come on down." We left the key in the mailbox with a note for the landlord saying he could have all her stuff, and dropped the cat off at the Humane Society on the way to the airport. I don't know what happened to it after that.

What happened to Linda was that her sister, who was more together than it appeared, got her to enroll at U.C.L.A. She took a fashion design course and now works with a designer in L.A. Most of the stuff you see with the Carol Valdy label is really hers, Linda's, and she travels all over Europe checking out the latest fashions, buying samples. When she wrote at Christmas, which is the only time I hear from her now, she said she was actually thinking of marrying this guy she'd been seeing for years and maybe even having a baby, if it's not too late.

"If we have a boy," she wrote," I'll call him Elvis, of course."

Mike calls this morning, just as I'm having my second cup of coffee, while the girls get their stuff together.

"Hey, what's this? I'll be there in a few hours."

"I know, but the weatherman is predicting a snowstorm this afternoon. I just wanted to make sure you were leaving early enough."

"In about half an hour. I'm just going to drop the girls off now. I should be there by one o'clock or so."

"Katherine, what about my coming there instead?"

"Mike, we've got the concert tickets and all. What is it? Don't you want me to come?"

"Of course I do. It's just, well, you know . . . "

I can see his hands, small for a man's and sinewy, fiddling with the phone cord or his watchband, twisting it the way he does, the receiver cradled on his shoulder.

"Yeah, I know. I'll be careful. See ya." I try to keep my tone light. There isn't much I can say, after all, at that distance, over the phone.

"Okay, I'll have the coffee on."

There's this little pause then, as if he wants to say something else and then thinks better of it, so he just hangs up. And it's as if I can see him, all of a sudden, in a kitchen I've never even seen, pacing around the way he does at my place, picking things up, straightening, rearranging. His hands were the first thing I noticed about him, their fine, almost-womanly shape, their movement. He has a thin scar on his right middle finger where his sister closed the car door on it when he was eight. I remember how I liked him at first because he was dark and sort of skittery in all the ways that David was blond and solid and comfortable. I thought this meant I was progressing somehow, getting over it, over the divorce.

Now I don't know. Now, I think maybe you never get over anything, you just find a way of carrying it as gently as possible. Now I just see Mike, dark and familiar, standing by the phone, which I imagine to be a plain black wall model, near the fridge. It's got one of those plastic memo pads beneath it and he's taken the pen from its holder, but he's not writing anything. He's just standing there, twiddling the pen in his fingers, staring at the phone. As if, if he keeps staring hard enough, he can will it not to ring.

CHICKEN 'N' RIBS

Lydia Robertson doesn't know what to call this, this *feeling* that comes over her these days, though by now she knows it well enough to recognize how it starts. With a little tickle at the back of her nose, up in that thin spot, there, between her eyes. Like a sneeze, only that's never what happens. Instead it's as if she's going to burst into tears for no reason and then it starts spreading, all through her, this, this *whatever*, like a blush or a hot flash (though surely she's still a bit young for that) and then . . .

Lydia clenches her fists and shoves them deeper into the pockets of her jacket, a taut, dark woman, her body kept wiry by hard work and anger. This is ridiculous. She and the kids are standing in line, waiting for a table, at the Swiss Chalet, for chrissake. *Not now* she pleads. But she knows it won't do any good.

She turns to the people who have just bunched up behind her as more people join the lineup. A woman and man, two kids much younger than her own. The woman is wearing a green sweater, the exact same shade of green as her eyes. It makes them look enormous. Like oceans, it seems to Lydia, so deep that the flecks of amber shining in them could be the lights of a drowned city still alive beneath the waves.

Lydia's own eyes flood with tears. She can't help herself.

"That sweater's perfect for you," she murmurs to the woman. "It's the exact same shade as your eyes. It lights up your whole face. In fact . . . " Lydia feels the words stirring in some place within her she didn't know existed and like someone carried away by love, she wants them to say something big and memorable. Though by the time they reach her lips, of course, they've already begun to shrink, abashed by the space the other woman's surprised expression has opened for them.

"In fact," Lydia hears them limping into the air, "your eyes light up this whole restaurant."

Idiot.

"Mother!" Lydia's daughter Karen prods her arm. "C'mon, the table's ready."

Lydia turns to follow the waitress, just as the husband leans towards his wife, his eyes still on Lydia, and one of the kids pipes up, "What did that lady say, Mommy, wha . . . "

"Really, Mother." Karen waits till they're seated and the waitress has spread out the placemats with the menu printed on them. "What were you trying to do back there?"

"Pay a simple compliment. It's a nice sweater."

"Are you serious? I thought you were making fun of her. Look at the pants she's got on with it!"

Lydia refuses to look.

"You mean you don't even *know* her?" Tony looks from his sister to his mother as if he suspects there's a joke he's not quite getting. "Jeez, Mom, you're weird."

Beside her, Richard, her oldest, slips his arm around her shoulder. "C'mon guys. Be nice."

He pulls out his wallet, leaning closer to her, laughing. "Now, Mom. No more talking to strangers and I'll buy you a beer. Promise?"

Lydia laughs, too, though she hates this snotty, smart-ass tone the kids take with her these days. It seems to be part of it somehow, part of this stupid feeling. Even her own kids can see she's acting like an asshole. *Jesus, Lydia.*

She's relieved when the waitress arrives to take their order. *But christ*, she thinks to herself, *look at the woman.* Unlike most of the girls who work here, she's older, easily Lydia's age. Though it could be the outfit. The girlish, scooped-neck, puffed-sleeve white blouse, and short, full jumper laced tightly under the breasts looks ridiculous if you're not five foot five inches, blonde, one hundred and ten pounds and under twenty-one. And their waitress is tired, too, and nervous. She has to ask Tony three times whether he wants baked or french-fried potatoes.

"Been a long day?" Lydia asks.

The woman's face opens in a grin. "Has it ever! This is my first weekend. Maybe I'm just too old for this. I don't know how these kids even manage, really."

Lydia pats her arm, ignoring Karen's stare. "Don't worry. You're doing fine. Just take your time."

"Yeah, I wish I could," the woman laughs as she turns to the booth behind her where a man is frantically waving his water glass.

"Are you planning to get to know *everyone* in here tonight?" Karen asks. "Can't you just enjoy yourself."

"I *am* enjoying myself. Jesus, it doesn't hurt to make some human contact, you know. Just you wait till you've worked in one of these places."

Oh, sure, Lydia, that's really convincing. Since when did blathering like an idiot to people you don't even know and couldn't care less about become your idea of a good time? Jesus, get serious.

And yet the strange thing is that Lydia doesn't feel unhappy. It's just that enjoyment seems too flat, too smug a word. *Overwhelmed* is what she *feels*, really, but overwhelmed by what? Love? Joy? This desire to reach out and hug – yes, hug – strangers as she would her own children, for no reason at all?

Lydia looks around her at the fake-oak beams, the fake wagon wheels suspended from the ceiling, each of their ten spokes holding an orange-shaded lantern which exudes a fake candle-like glow. The wood around the windows has little flowers carved in it. Fake shutters. She imagines a massive factory and huge machines, like cookie cutters, stamping fake Swiss flowers into an endless assembly line of fake-wood panels destined for branch franchises in cities and towns all over North America. Hell, the world. They've probably got these same restaurants in Tokyo and Nairobi. Lydia tries to picture it: tall African women or tiny Japanese in a place exactly like this, dressed like women they have never seen. Women *no one* has ever seen, really, all of it the creation of some Madison Avenue imagination.

So why does it happen here, then? If what she is having is some sort of *spiritual experience* (and this is a phrase that Lydia resists even more strenuously than she resists the experience itself, though like the experience, it rises, unbidden to her mind), *if* she is having such an experience, what is it about the Swiss Chalet, of all places, that brings it on?

Even the food, which is just now arriving, gets to her. Each plate is arranged exactly the same with its tidy heap of french fries, the perfectly browned quarter-chicken, the carefully toasted roll, all as precise as the flowers stamped out on the shutters. Beside each plate is a small bowl of barbecue sauce and a side plate for the paper cuplets of ketchup, two bigger ones of sour cream for Karen's baked potato.

Who does all this? Lydia wonders. *How many people do they have out there doing nothing else for eight, ten hours but arranging these plates?* It touches her (and at the same time she recoils, embarrassed, really embarrassed, by such a touch) that all this immense organization is there for her. For all of them. The place is packed tonight. It's the last Friday of the month, payday, and everyone, like Lydia, has at least a few dollars to spend on a meal out. And, sure enough, she feels a sudden gush of love for the people around her, hard workers like herself, enjoying a few minutes with their families, enjoying the food.

Good god, Lydia, you could write the frigging commercials. The food is overpriced, overspiced, the waitresses are overworked. This is a fast-food franchise you're in here; one step, barely, up from McDonald's, for chrissake.

At the far end of the restaurant, four aisles to Lydia's left, is an open space filled with tables instead of booths.

Along one side, several tables have been pulled together to accommodate what looks like a large family party, though the people seem to be somewhat overdressed for the Swiss Chalet, the men in dark suits, the women in flowery dresses which are still too light for the early spring weather outside. One couple in particular seems to be the centre of everyone's attention, though Lydia can't really see their faces between the heads and shoulders of the people sitting opposite them.

She can see the man sitting to their left, though. A boy, really, red-haired and thin-faced. High cheekbones. From where she is, Lydia can't quite make out the freckles that cover those cheekbones, but she knows they're there, just as she knows that his eyes are grey, shallow and protected by lids that are surprisingly heavy for the rest of his face.

At least this is what Lydia imagines she knows in the brief instant before he leans out of her sight towards someone at the end of the table. He reminds her of her husband, Ken. In fact, it could even *be* her husband Ken, unchanged, unapologetic, too stupid to recognize her or his own children just a few tables away. For all she knows (or cares, she tells herself), it could even be another son of Ken's, while Ken himself is just out of sight, fat (she hopes) and grey, sitting with some faded blonde he met on the road somewhere, a few hours after he walked out of their house on Palace Road fifteen years ago.

She was twenty-one at the time. Richard was four, Karen, two and a half; Tony wasn't even crawling yet. Ken was working as an installer for Kemco fencing; on weekends he played bass guitar with a bar band called The Sir John A's; he still talked of cutting a record someday. But that day, June 15, he left for work as usual. Lydia thinks she remembers handing him his lunchbox at the door, though it's all kind of blurry, because she was also trying to get the kids fed and dressed in time to be at the bus stop by 8:15 in the morning. Tony had an ear infection. She'd called the doctor's office first thing and they'd said if she could have him there by 8:45 A.M., the doctor could probably take a look. He was booked solid the rest of the day.

When she got back to the house at ten o'clock, Ken's lunchbox was on the table. At first she'd thought he'd forgotten it; then she thought maybe he'd taken sick or been hurt. But the car wasn't in the driveway and he didn't answer when she called. It was Richard who saw the note, propped against the lunchbox.

Dear Liddie,

Look, I'm sorry, but I can't take anymore of this. I've got to get out while I can. I hope what's inside will get you through the worst of it. You can tell the kids whatever you want. I won't be back. Don't try to find me. Please.

love, Ken

Inside the lunchbox was a plastic bag full of marijuana and ten 100 dollar bills.

"Anything else here?" Their waitress looks even more exhausted than she did a few minutes ago. Her mascara's smudged, too, as if she's been crying. Lydia fights the desire to grab her by the elbow and steer her out of the place, waving away the indignant manager. *Christ, there should be laws against this kind of bullshit.*

She looks down at the finger bowl of warm water which the waitress is placing in front of her. There's a tiny sliver of lemon floating in it. Lydia imagines a room heaped with lemons, a slim, dark girl slivering the peel away . . . *No, there must be a machine . . .*

"Just coffee for me, please," she says, keeping her voice hard, impersonal. "Tony? Richard?"

The boys both order apple pie and ice cream. Karen is on a diet. The waitress turns away, already running, and barely escapes colliding with a busboy. Lydia looks over at Karen, catching her eye, hoping to god her expression is as haughty as her daughter's.

For the next few weeks, Lydia got up as she always had, as soon as the kids called at 6:30 A.M. She'd feed them and make some coffee. Then she'd fill the bathtub, adding bubble bath, maybe some food colouring. The kids loved the idea of coloured baths, so she let them experiment. A violent fuchsia one morning, a gross baby-shit yellow another. Then while Karen and Richard played in the tub and Tony bounced in the doorway in his Jolly Jumper, Lydia sat on the toilet seat and smoked a large joint while she drank her coffee. She rolled them the size of cigars, the hell with making the stuff last. Later, in an underwater haze, she'd dress the kids, pack up lemonade, sandwiches, diapers, carrot sticks, pails and shovels and head off for the park.

The place swam with children and hers jumped right into things. They got along fine, but the other women avoided her. She thought maybe they could tell somehow, as if Ken's ditching her was something catching, like those creepy things – scabies or lice – that kids bring home from school. Most of the time she didn't really give a shit. Most of the time she was glad if she could just sit there, smooth-faced, smiling, hoping the dope would hold her until nap-time.

When it rained, she took the kids to the mall, wandering for hours, in and out of the stores, letting them have dozens of rides on the mechanical horse at Loblaws. Then she'd take them to the Jiffy Snack Bar for chips and gravy and chocolate milk shakes. Comfort food. Like the stuff she made them for supper at night. Wieners and beans. Kraft dinner. Jello. Easy to cook, easy to eat.

It was usually then that they'd ask where Daddy was. Right from the start Lydia was determined not to pull any punches. He'd gone away for good, why pretend he hadn't? So that's what she told them. "Daddy isn't coming back." "But why, Mommy, why?" *Because he's a no-good, chicken-shit, asshole, that's why.* She didn't say that, of course, though it was true, obviously. She even kept the note for them to read when they learned how, but by that time they seemed to have forgotten. Later, as they reached their teens, Karen and Richard used to read it over and over until it became grubby and wrinkled like a dollar bill. Tony never even asked. Now, nobody does.

And it serves you right, too, fuck-head. Lydia raises her beer bottle in a jaunty sort of toast. None of the kids catch her, thank god.

23

She sneaks a glance at Karen, who is still picking at the last of her baked potato, carefully avoiding the skin, which she hates. She has red hair like her father's, but paler and curly. Lydia can't remember now if it was always curly or if it got that way because Karen spends so much time around the water. She wants to be a marine biologist. Her hair makes Lydia think of that picture of Venus on a shell coming out of the ocean, only with Karen it should be a mermaid. If the artist had ever painted a mermaid, Karen would be it.

Lydia reaches for Karen's hand.

"What?"

What? "Oh, nothing; I just love you, that's all."

"Really," Karen pulls her hand away, but gently, she's laughing, "not here, Mother, control yourself. Tony's right. You're getting very weird."

When she looks at her own hand, there, on the tabletop beside Karen's, Lydia is ashamed, as she always is, by how old it looks, how, how *forgotten*. What's left of the polish she put on last week looks like rust, most of it peeled away by now. The soap at the hospital is murder on it anyway, she doesn't know why she bothers. And besides, her cuticles are so thick and uneven that polish hardly improves anything. Like a child's fingers, hers, stubby and unkempt. Except that the back of the hand – the thick, raised veins and the dry, cracked skin – is that of an old woman. An old, dried-up witch. Who'd want to hold a hand like that? Lydia cramps her fingers into a fist.

"Excuse me." The waitress sets a cup of coffee down in front of her, slopping some of it into the saucer as she does so. Even Lydia can see that this woman is a loser, she'll never make it. Her hands are as dry and sinewy as Lydia's; there's a burn blister on the back, a red bracelet of smaller marks dotted around her wrist. Lydia can imagine what she's like in the kitchen where they pick up their orders – a walking disaster. No wonder the other waitresses seem to avoid her.

And then suddenly, without warning, it happens again. Lydia wants to kiss those burn marks, slowly, one by one. She wants to hold that hand between her two and rub it as she used to rub the pain from her children's fingers when they played outside too long in the snow, their hands numb beneath woollen mittens.

Jesus, Lydia, get a grip. Who the hell do you think you are anyway, Mother Theresa?

Laughter from the table at the other side of the room turns the heads of everyone in the restaurant. A stout, grey man (though not, Lydia can see, that much older than herself) is tapping his glass with his spoon in the traditional manner of someone at a wedding party about to make a speech.

He is going to make a speech.

It *is* a wedding party.

"Can you believe this?" Karen can't, obviously. "They're having a wedding reception *here*. God, this is bizarre."

"Makes sense to me." Richard is mock-serious – "I mean, you can't get big enough tables at McDonald's."

"Shut up you guys. We're eating here, aren't we?" As soon as the words are out, of course, Lydia regrets them.

"Yeah, Mom, but no one's getting married" – Karen takes it as a joke – "and if you're saying I have to have my wedding reception at the Swiss Chalet, then I just won't bother with a wedding at all."

Don't then, for fuck sake. There's lots of times I wish I hadn't.

There's a moment when Lydia thinks she has said this out loud. Then another when she feels as if her head is being held underwater, while the words roar in her ears. When she surfaces again, though, Karen and Richard are still carrying on.

". . . no, the Ponderosa," Karen demands, laughing, "and four bridesmaids; two to hold my train while I stand in line for my steak – I'll have to carry my own tray – one to hold my bouquet and another to get my salad at the salad bar."

"Where over fifty country-fresh selections are available daily," Richard adds.

"Right."

Their voices come from a long distance. At the wedding table, the stout man finishes his speech and Lydia catches the brief blur of a bridal kiss, framed by dark shoulders. She thinks she sees the tip of a bridal bouquet – roses and baby's breath – on the table near a bowl of barbecue sauce. Suddenly, it seems, all the men are sporting blue carnations; some of the women wear big hats, the kind you imagine when you think of garden parties, loaded with flowers.

When she looks at her own wedding pictures these days (which is not very often, but more often than she'd care to admit), Lydia has the oddest feeling that the people in them have changed. For years after he left, she studied

Ken's face and her own, looking for clues and finding none. Nothing but tight smiles and the usual glazed looks that come from too many flashbulbs. Or, in Ken's case, too much beer. Her own blurred pallor came from the fact that she was sneaking off to puke every ten minutes, since she was, of course, three months pregnant.

What she sees now, though, is fear. More of it every time she opens the album. Stunned with it, both of them. Like children at a school play, fighting to keep their eyes front, not to look off-stage, search out the teacher in the wings, ready to give them, any moment now (*please, please*), the line they have forgotten.

And yet, she can't remember *feeling* afraid at all. Can't remember feeling anything, really. Not even when she told her parents, after she knew for sure she was pregnant, in the kitchen after dinner. Not even in the silence that followed, the sounds of her brothers playing in the driveway suddenly rising through it, painful and irritating, too, like a longing for something she knew she couldn't have, her father slumped in his chair, her mother's hands fiddling with spoons, with the lid of the sugar bowl. Not even then, when it hit her there was nothing they could do. Their anger and their disappointment couldn't touch her anymore. She was on her own.

And later, when Ken left, there just wasn't time. After a month of sitting stoned in the park every day, stunned, stupid with heat and fatigue, when it finally, finally sank in that what she was telling the kids was really true – Daddy wasn't coming back, ever – she was just too tired to be angry or hurt. Too out of it to know what to be frightened of. She remembers coming up, like someone surfacing from a plunge that had taken her deeper than she'd expected, but admitting no danger, shrugging it off. Fuck the world, she'd show them. Throwing the rest of the dope in the garbage and calling home.

"Hi, Mom? It's me, Lydia. Look, Ken's left me, the jerk . . . no, no I don't know and I don't care. Good riddance to bad rubbish as far as I'm concerned. But I want to go back to school . . . I know, I know, but it's different now. There's these night courses I can take, one night a week. If you and Dad could take the kids . . . "

"Well, I'll see, Liddie. I'll have to ask your father."

For chrissake, Mother. It's me, Lydia. Your one and only daughter, remember? Jesus.

It took her an hour, every goddamn Wednesday, just to get out to her parents' place by bus. Tony in the carrier on her back, one hand for each of the other kids, Richard and Karen fighting over who would carry her books. Back downtown to the high school, two hours of classes and then the whole trip, again, in reverse. Usually the kids were asleep when she got back, so she'd take a cab. Ignore her father's asshole comments about champagne style on a beer budget. It was the money Ken had left her, after all. Her "luxury account" she called it. Ha. Ha. Course fees and textbooks, cab fares for times like this or when she had more groceries than she could carry. A haircut once. She kept what was left of the money in the lunchbox in the closet. She couldn't bank it because of Mothers' Allowance.

By the time she started on her nursing diploma, Karen and Richard were both in school and the woman upstairs was willing to take Tony. Her cousin Lee lent her the money so she didn't have to get a student loan. That way, Mothers' Allowance didn't have to know. Her social worker had told her that they cut payments to women who were "not mothering full time," as she put it. Two years later, the day Tony started kindergarten, Lydia started full time at the General. Three years after that, she'd managed to pay Lee back everything she owed her. The next year, they finally moved to a bigger apartment.

And that's all she can remember. That's it. Everything else is a blur, speeded up, like a video on fast forward, a cartoon jumble of patients, paperwork, cooking, shopping, laundry, cleaning, worrying that one of the kids would get sick when she was working days or that the babysitter would ignore them when she was working nights, trying to save enough to send them to university. Her one and only life, whizzing by her as if, after Ken left, it had no time for her. Her own life.

"Spiritual experience." Hell, what a laugh. Burnout, more likely. Maybe she's going to flip out, like Sonya Peters, the head nurse on neo-natal, who woke up one day to find herself in a motel outside of Edmonton, with the cops banging on her door. Turns out she'd just walked out of the hospital, got in her car and started driving. Been gone for over a week when they found her. Couple of shock treatments, a few months of tranqs and she was back at work, good as new.

Yeah Lydia, think about it. Take some of your sick-time. Buy a few new sweaters. Go south. Don't make more of this than it is.

And yet. She remembers reading somewhere that women in the Middle Ages used to take themselves off to convents sometimes. Women her age, married women, the few who survived childbearing and hard work and their own husbands, used to become nuns, abbesses even, founding religious orders, giving the last of their lives to God.

To themselves, more like it, Lydia figures. A few last years of peace and quiet they'd at least know about before an eternity of nothingness. What else could it be? Surely they didn't have these gushes of, of *feeling* for anyone, God included. Not after the lives they led. What kind of sense would *that* make?

Forget it, Lydia. It's just your Mother Theresa complex again. Get a grip. Really.

While Lydia, Karen and Richard finish their coffee, Tony takes off to play a few video games at the Gameskeeper, which is just next door to the restaurant. Even the third time around, it's strange to watch him go off like that, her last, able to manage on his own. Strange to find herself sitting here, talking so easily with the other two, Richard full of his plans for university in September, Karen still agonizing over the last of her high school credits.

Around them, other groups sit talking, too. Mostly families of one sort or another. A husband and wife with a couple of kids. Lots of women like her, on their own with them. More men, she's noticed lately, weekend fathers some of them, or single parents, too. Suddenly, she wants to stand up in front of everyone, tap her coffee cup with her spoon, make an announcement.

"I'm Lydia Robertson. These are my two eldest children, Richard, who plans to become a mechanical engineer, and Karen, my only daughter, who will study marine biology. Save the whales, maybe, or the whole

ocean. I have raised these two, along with their younger brother, Tony, on my own for the past fifteen years, while at the same time finishing my high school education and becoming a nurse. I am now a supervisor of nursing in the OB *unit at the General. I want you to know that I have accomplished all this, alone, with minimal help from my family and without any assistance, other than the obvious and easily performed biological one, from my husband, Ken, a no-good bastard who, who . . . "*

At this point Lydia's speech, even in her imagination, breaks down. She knows the next line, all right. By heart. She can hear herself, her own voice, inside her head, repeating the words she has said so many times before, but suddenly they sound distant and mechanical, something she memorized years ago and never really listened to again. You push the button marked "Ken" and out they come, like those set-speeches people fill a room with when their minds are on automatic.

"Ken," she says, out loud this time, but softly, under her breath, so that even in her ears it sounds like a sigh escaping, tight and scared, the sigh of someone who's been hard done by, the sigh of someone holding on, holding back. "Ken," she tries again, a little louder, as if she were actually speaking to someone. A real person, with a life of his own somewhere, and a job and maybe even a family, maybe still playing with some bar band, the same old songs, still kind of hoping to make it someday, but knowing, too, that he never would. A person she could forgive, if she wanted to. If she wanted to get on with it.

"Ken."

It may be that Karen and Richard hear her this time, for they turn their heads, but just then the wedding party prepares to leave. Chairs are shoved back and people stand awkwardly now, as if suddenly aware of the attention focused on them. Two men discuss the bill, a little too loudly.

Lydia still can't see the bride and groom. The red-haired boy and another, smaller version stand in front of them, laughing. High school kids, probably, all four of them.

Dear teacher: My daughter Selma will be absent tomorrow. She's getting married.

The two boys start elbowing each other, laughing. The older one pushes his brother into the chairs, as a woman's voice rises.

The bride's – yelling at her kid brothers.

Then Lydia gets a glimpse of her face.

No, for chrissake. She's yelling at her sons.

"Well, I'll be . . . "

And at that moment, the bride, whose short, grey hair puffs out absurdly from under a bright blue hat, raises her eyes from the boys, as if in answer to Lydia. And Lydia imagines – no, believes – that she smiles directly at her, as one woman often smiles at another over children's heads, a smile that explains somehow, by gently refusing the need to explain at all, the incongruity of her situation.

And Lydia knows, then, exactly what to do.

"You pay the bill," she says to Richard, "I'll get Tony."

But she is not, of course, going to get Tony. Next to the Gameskeeper is a tiny flower shop, a hole in the wall that Lydia enters now and, in a blur and the click of a credit card, buys the entire stock.

"Do you want them wrapped?"

"No, just pile them here," Lydia holds out her arms, laughing.

Keeps on laughing as the clerk opens the door for her. As Karen, too surprised to do anything else, opens the door to the Swiss Chalet. As she steps inside, her arms extended, filled with irises, mauve freesia, daffodils, pink daisies, red tulips, blue carnations and yellow roses, laughing and laughing as she enters the small pause where everyone seems to be waiting for her.

FASHION ACCENTS

I have to start this story by telling you about those crinkly scarves that were all the rage that summer. The first time I saw them, in our backyard – when they came swirling down like a cloud of giant, crazy butterflies from Stella Simpson's outstretched hands – wasn't the first time I'd ever seen them, but it was the first time they mattered, if you know what I mean. Before that they'd been something I wanted, really wanted, in Kresge's, but my mother said they were foolishness at that price and what was wrong with the scarves Aunt Edna had brought me from Florida.

The scarves Aunt Edna brought me from Florida were shiny and scratchy and ugly. You couldn't knot them casually at the throat the way the magazines were

showing so that they peeked slyly out of the collar of
your blouse, "a bright note of sophisticated colour."
These scarves were made of some soft material, per-
manently set into tiny accordion pleats that fanned out at
the ends when you tied them around your neck. They
came in solid, adult colours. Navy, bright red, turquoise,
lime green, lemon yellow and a strong, true pink like the
lipstick my mother wore and that I wore, too, for the
hour after I got home from school before she got home
from work. Seeing them float down to me from Stella –
as she leaned out her bedroom window and said, "Here,
would you like these?" in a way that was as casual, as
generous, as her hands – was like being in a dream.
There was one of every colour they had and she gave
them to me because she liked me, she thought I was cute,
she wanted to be my friend.

The Simpsons lived in Apartment Four which was
directly above ours and was the exact same size – living
room-dining room, kitchen, two bedrooms and bath. The
difference was that theirs had six people in it – Mr.
Simpson, Stella, their three little boys and Stella's
mother, Mrs. Jackson. You weren't supposed to do this.
Mr. McIntosh, the superintendent, liked to keep things
under control. The only reason they'd got in at all was
that Stella had not told him she was pregnant. She'd
also said that her mother was only staying a couple of
weeks.

That had been over a year ago. Mrs. Jackson still slept
on a pull-out bed in the living room and kept her clothes
in the closet of the room the boys shared.

"And they won't throw us out now," Stella said to my
mother, laughing. "You know how it is. Possession is
nine-tenths of the law. We've got our rights."

I could tell by the way my mother squinched her lips ever so slightly that she did not agree. She disapproved of lying in any form and she had said to my father that she thought it was "terrible, making that poor woman sleep on that old roll-out. They treat her like a slave, really. You can bet it's not Stella who's raising those kids. I've never seen her lift a finger. They're not bad boys, I'm not saying that, but they're too much for anyone that age."

She also meant they were too much, period. Too many. The two oldest boys, who were seven and four, drove their tricycles up and down the hall, which my brother and I had never been allowed to do. The baby, who was crawling now, went around sucking on a soother, wearing only a diaper. Their door was almost always open and the kids ran in and out as they felt like it. What my mother meant was that the Simpsons brought the place down a notch or two, which was a lot, considering. She meant that because of the Simpsons the walls were even smearier than they used to be, the smell a little sadder, more permanent.

On the other hand, Ronnie and Ryan Simpson were company for my brother Carl, and Mrs. Jackson was always there if we needed anything after school. My mother worked as a receptionist for Dr. Watson. My dad, who was an installer for Bell, picked her up after work, but he couldn't always be sure what time he'd get there, especially if his last job was out in the suburbs, so they hardly ever got home before six. I was supposed to keep an eye on Carl, put the potatoes on and set the table. That was okay. I liked having the place to myself. I turned the radio up as loud as I felt like and practised jiving, using the kitchen door as a partner. Sometimes I went up to see Stella.

"Hi there! Want a coffee?" was what she usually said when I appeared at the door. She never got up and fussed the way my mother did, pulling out a chair, getting down cups. She'd just sort of wave in the general direction of the stove where the coffee pot was and I'd help myself.

Stella was always at the kitchen table. Usually she had on a loose, long half-nightgown, half-bathrobe sort of thing, which was nothing like anything my mother wore. Her makeup mirror was always on the table in front of her, surrounded by tweezers and manicure scissors, pots of eyeshadow, glass bottles filled with nail polish, nail polish remover and perfume, cans of hairspray, ashtrays, cigarettes and mugs of half-finished coffee. There'd be at least one cigarette (besides the one she had in her mouth or her hand) burning somewhere and Stella was always, always putting on makeup or taking it off, plucking her eyebrows, teasing her hair, shaving her legs or painting her nails.

She was a large, blonde woman who talked a lot about losing weight, though she never did as long as I knew her. I couldn't imagine her thin – she wouldn't have been Stella – anymore than I could imagine her pretty in the way the women in the magazines were pretty. Stella's nose was too large, her eyes too close together, her mouth was crooked. But she was beautiful, Stella. Even then I knew that her beauty had to do with what was called style. I also knew that I needed some badly, since I was not going to be beautiful in the normal, easy way that some of my girlfriends seemed to manage. Marion Patterson, for instance, didn't need to worry about how she looked, even at the end of gym class, in those ugly, blue gymsuits, with her hair all mussed up. But I was awkward and skinny; my hair was too straight to be left casually alone. I needed style. At the time I thought it was something simple, something you could learn by watching.

So I'd sit down across from Stella and take a couple of drags off the nearest cigarette. She never offered me a whole one; I think it may have been one of her few rules, but she always positioned the ashtray so that one was easily within reach.

"Have you tried this Lucky Lady Lavender, yet?" she'd say, pushing a bottle of nail polish towards me. "I just got it this morning. I want to see what it looks like on you. It makes my hands look too yellow, I think."

I'd try the nail polish and Stella would lean back in her chair, take a long drag off her cigarette and let the smoke out slowly. "Try it with the lipstick," she'd say, "and just a touch of this on your eyelids. Mom, what do you think of this shade on Brenda?"

Mrs. Jackson was a soft, fat woman, I could never tell how old. My mother was right, she did do most of the work, but that seemed to be understood between them, between her and Stella. And even I could see that this understanding grew out of love, though it wasn't the kind of love my mother had for me.

"Well, I don't know," she'd say, coming up behind Stella's chair and staring hard at me. "I think the lipstick's *too* pink, don't you? With that lilac especially. Where's that sweet shade you got at Zeller's last week?" And Stella would jump up and run to her bedroom and come back with more tubes and bottles. Mrs. Jackson herself wore loose cotton housedresses, furry slippers and no makeup at all, but she seemed as intimate with the nuances of fashion vocabulary as Stella was. You'd think it was the only thing they ever talked about.

My mother was wrong about the boys, too. They were all over Stella. Or would have been if she'd let them.

"Wait a sec, now, you'll smear my lipstick," she'd cry. "Just let it set and I'll give you a big pink kiss." And they'd stand there, the only time I ever saw them quiet, until she scooped them up and covered their faces with lip-prints while they kicked and screamed with delight. The baby, Sam, climbed up and down off her lap twenty times an hour. I never heard her raise her voice to any of them, ever, though she did things that would have given my mother apoplexy, like letting the boys have sips of coffee or putting a couple inches of Coke in the baby's bottle.

Around five or so Mr. Simpson would arrive. He was a fine-boned, little man who still appears in my mind whenever I hear the word "natty." He had dark hair and a crisp, dark moustache and, unlike any other man I knew at the time, wore suits to work. A dark blue one, a soft "charcoal," and a tweedy, blue-grey that Stella called "heather," and with which he wore a dark blue tie with a matching handkerchief in his breast pocket. He had a large assortment of ties, always with matching handkerchiefs, but this one was my favourite. I agreed with Stella that it really brought out the colour of his eyes.

Mr. Simpson was the manager of the Princess Theatre downtown, a dumpy little second-run place, I know now, though at the time it seemed very glamorous to me. He referred to his job as "the entertainment business" and was always talking about what was coming and who was in it, in the flat, intimate way of someone who has specialized inside information. He usually came home just to grab something between the matinee and the early show. There was always a plate for him in the oven and he'd eat standing up, leaning against the fridge, talking to Stella.

They talked about bills to be paid, about how much money was in the account and whether they could afford to get that chair they'd seen at Reid's, about how Ronnie had been caught peeing in Mrs. Henderson's flowerbed again. They talked about these things casually and without any apparent embarrassment at my listening. In my house, such conversations were private family affairs, but the Simpsons not only didn't ignore my presence, they actually *included* it, occasionally asking my opinion and listening to my answers. In my mind, this fit with the open door and the fact that no one ever ate regular meals at their place and Stella's long gowns and her throwing the scarves out the window. It summed them up, in a way. It was what they *were*, the Simpsons, which was different, a whole lot different, from *my* family.

My parents were planning and saving to buy a house in the suburbs. I heard them talking about it in low voices after I'd gone to bed.

"We've got to get out before she gets much older," my mother would say. "This neighbourhood and all, Doug, you know what I mean. And they can't share that bedroom much longer. She'll be fourteen soon."

And my father would say, "Yes, yes, Frances, I know. Let's just see what we get with the contract this fall. It's looking good, it's . . . "

And then they would seem to lower their voices even further, or a good song would come on my transistor and I would have to pull the blankets over my head so I could turn up the volume without Carl telling on me.

The last thing I did before I fell asleep every night was to set my alarm for 6:30 A.M. This was so I could have at least fifteen minutes in the bathroom before everyone else got up. I spent this time squeezing pimples, parting my hair on the other side, checking my breasts for enlargement, my underarms and pubic area for signs of hair. There was an odd mix of eagerness and fear in this ritual – like the way I pulled down my underpants, at the slightest twinge of a cramp, to see if I'd finally started getting my period – as if I expected these changes to arrive without warning, overnight. In a way, I think that is exactly what I *did* expect.

I always locked the bathroom door, of course, and this drove my mother nuts.

"Brenda, you've been in there long enough. Your father and I have to get to work. You're not the only person in the world, you know," she would say. I hated that. I hated the way she acted as if I were still a selfish child. It never seemed to occur to her that I just didn't want her around.

My mother's morning routine was brisk and disgusting. As soon as I opened the door, she would push past me to the toilet, pee, flush and step immediately into the bathtub, turning on the tap as she did so. We didn't have a shower, so my mother would sort of half squat to splash her armpits, breasts and crotch, soap them and splash again. Then she'd step out of the tub, towel lightly, dab on deodorant and talcum and push me gently out of the way while she brushed her teeth, applied lipstick and fluffed her hair. The whole operation took less time than it would have taken Stella to paint one nail or put the outliner on her lips with the lip pencil before she even started to fill them in. On many mornings my mother's body exuded a ripe, sweetish smell that reminded me of vegetables that had been in the fridge too long. Much later, of course, I recognized this on my own body as the smell of sex. Then, it was almost embarrassing, too close for comfort. Like her breath on the back of my neck when she stood behind me at the bathroom mirror.

Stella smelled of cigarettes, coffee and some spicy perfume I have never been able to find anywhere. I think now that it came from what she was, like her gestures or her way of talking. She could talk to anyone in just the right way. She never, for instance, used that goo-goo voice that most adults have for children, even their own. She was just Stella talking to her kids. With Mr. Simpson, her voice was throaty, with a chuckle in it, as if they shared a joke that no one else got.

"The briefcase boy still got the hots for you?" Stella asks me.

She means Gary Barlow, this jerky little browner who keeps sending me notes in history class. He carries a briefcase and has this way of lining up his pens on his desk that makes me want to bump against it when I walk by, like I would if he were my brother, just to bug him. I don't want to have anything to do with him; I already get too many A's myself. I take a long drag off a cigarette before I answer.

"Yeah, and he's asked me to the dance on Friday night."

"You gonna go?"

"Stella! He's a total dork."

"So what are you gonna do then, sit home all night? He won't exactly be the only boy at the dance, you know. You never know what will happen."

Stella and I are painting our nails, pausing every so often to take a sip of coffee, flex our fingers, tilt our heads, study the effect. My mother has told me that I shouldn't hurt that nice boy's feelings, and it isn't as if they're lining up to ask me out, is it? I already know that she would regard Stella's advice as what she calls, vaguely, "using boys," though for me it has the effect of making Gary Barlow and my going out with him incidental, like the high, slightly sickly smell of the wet polish.

And then it evaporates. Stella reaches for my hand.

"Oh, say now, that is perfect. But not with that green sweater. I've got just the thing – " And she tips her chair back, leaning dangerously, making it look easy, the heel of her right hand pressed against the table to balance her, a cigarette still between her fingers, the left reaching back to a pile of clothes, handing me a soft pink blouse. "Here, try it with this. It's way too small for me anymore. You might as well have it."

Of course, I wore Stella's blouse to the dance (with my navy skirt and the navy, crinkly scarf at the neck) and, of course, it all turned out okay. Gary was a not-bad dancer; Steve Anderson asked me out the next week. But all that probably could have happened anyway, without Stella. Despite my high marks and thin chest, I was destined to have as normal a life as any of us do. It was just that the way Stella talked to me made it seem suddenly possible, really possible, for me to see myself actually having such a life. This was what my mother couldn't give me, though later I would see that she'd wanted to. What I saw then, in Stella, was the only adult I'd met who hadn't forgotten everything I needed to know.

For one thing, she was much younger than my mother, she was twenty-eight. I could talk to Stella almost the way I talked to my girlfriends, and yet she was also an adult, with a husband and kids. Even her mother didn't seem to act like *her mother*, if you know what I mean.

And Stella had only been seventeen, just a few years older than I was, when Ronnie was born, whereas my mother had been twenty-nine when she'd had me. It seemed to me that these differences in their ages had tremendous implications. I was beginning to see that there were a lot of ways of doing things, of living, that I'd never really thought about. My parents made it seem like there was only one way and up until now I had accepted that, at the same time as it made me feel rather, well, *discouraged*. So when I say that Stella suddenly made my life seem possible, what I really mean, I guess, is *possibilities*, ways of getting on that I thought I could manage.

Stella and my mother are sitting at our kitchen table having coffee. They do this sometimes, especially on Saturday afternoons in the winter when my dad has taken the boys to a hockey game.

"It's the least you can do," my mother has said to him, "otherwise her two will be sitting in that dark, stuffy theatre all day watching goodness knows what."

But now she is talking to Stella as she talks to all her friends. Saying things like "Isn't that men for you," or "Kids, eh?" in this certain way she has, sighing or groaning or barking out this hard, little laugh that makes what she says sound idiotic and mysterious at the same time. On these occasions, I sit at the table between them, keeping quiet, listening, the way Ronnie does sometimes when Stella and I talk.

Today, my mother is telling Stella about the time she had when I was born. This is a story I've heard so often that it sounds remote and legendary now, like something in a book. I know every word she's going to use, every place she'll laugh or sigh. It's sort of like when she used to read to me as a little kid, the same book over and over until I could repeat it to myself, turning the pages, thinking I knew how to read.

"So I told Doug, there was no point in him hanging around. Fussing and fuming. You know how men are in hospitals. It's enough to drive you wild, even without a baby on the way. So I told him, 'Doug, it's going to be a while, now, you go on back to your work. Let me get on with mine.' "

My mother stops for a sip of coffee, as she always does at this point. Then the little laugh, the shrug of her shoulders.

"Of course, I didn't know then it was going to be so long. Two days, if you can believe it. They called him, naturally, when they thought they were going to lose her, but I didn't know that."

"Lose her?" Stella leans forward slightly, as everyone does at this point in the story, as if she's missed something, but I know what's coming next.

"Well, yes, after two days, when she finally got here" – my mother nods, now, at me – "she was more than a little out of shape. They said she'd never make it."

"You mean, they told you she was gonna die?" Stella's voice rises in a croak of disbelief, which is exactly what my mother wants.

"Well, that's what they said," she rolls her eyes, laughing. The way she would if she'd told you about some serviceman who'd wanted to charge an outrageous amount to fix the washing machine when any fool could see that all it needed was a couple of fifty-cent wires.

"That's what they said, of course. Doctors."

"Doctors." Like "men" or "kids," rolling her eyes again, pointing at me as if I were proof of something. As if anyone who couldn't understand that, couldn't understand anything.

My mother picks up her coffee mug, smiling.

Stella lights another cigarette from the one in her mouth, stubs out the first one and leans forward again.

"And after all that," she says, "you went on and had another one?" Somehow she makes it sound more like an accusation than a question.

"Well," says my mother, huffily, "these things happen. There's no sense dwelling on it."

"Jesus Christ" – Stella exhales a thin, urgent stream of smoke – "Jesus Christ. I screamed my head off for all three. Something like that'd be enough to make me keep my legs crossed the rest of my goddamned life."

My mother scrinches her lips up every so slightly.

"I'm not saying it didn't hurt," she says lightly. "But you know what they say – the most quickly forgotten pain in the world."

Stella stubs out her cigarette, folds the foil down over the rest of the pack, takes a last gulp of coffee.

"Well, I don't . . . " she begins, only what happens next is the sound of the car doors slamming in the driveway. My dad back with the boys. My mother looks up at the clock and then turns towards the door, just as they all come in, stamping their feet and throwing their mitts around. But there is a moment in there somewhere when I catch on Stella's face a look I've never seen on an adult's before, sort of stubborn and helpless at the same time, something I think I recognize from the playground or the classroom.

But then it disappears and Stella is just Stella again. Ronnie and Ryan crowd up to her and she starts kissing them all over, the way she always does.

The Simpsons lived upstairs for almost three years. There were lots of times when I wouldn't see Stella for weeks and then she'd come down and say, "How about a show tonight?" and we'd get all dressed up and go. We'd take a taxi, something I'd never done with anyone else, so that I know it's from Stella I have my love of arriving in one still, like a woman who's lived in taxicabs all her life. And because of Mr. Simpson we always got in free, sweeping past the ticket girl with one minute to go, Stella waving ("Hi Gracie, haven't you got that bun out of the oven yet?"), calling to Fred, the usher, to keep that door open one more minute while we got popcorn and Cokes,

blowing a kiss to Mr. Simpson who'd be talking on the
phone in his office, the whole place opening up to her,
everybody smiling and laughing as if they wanted to
applaud.

Of all the movies we saw together, I remember only
snippets, half-scenes. The part in *Where the Boys Are*
when Yvette Mimieux leaves the motel in a daze after
she's done it with some guy and gets hit by a car on the
highway. Her pale, pale face in the hospital bed. Stella
and me clutching each other. Stella and me sobbing
along with everyone else at the end of *Imitation of Life*,
all those flowers, Susan Kohner fighting her way through
the crowd, throwing herself, sobbing, on her mother's
coffin. *Maudlin*, I can say now, of course, when I see the
reruns on TV. But that doesn't change anything. And I'm
not embarrassed to turn and see myself in that old
theatre, clutched in Stella's arms, bawling my eyes out.
They seemed so vulnerable, those women on the screen,
and so grown-up at the same time, running towards or
away from some huge, terrible event. I suppose it was
really myself I was crying for then, wanting my own life
to be as huge and as terrible as theirs.

And then she was gone. For good.

"Walked out on that poor man," my mother said, "that
poor man and those three little boys without so much as
a backward glance." She made it sound grand and
sweeping, like the way I thought of Stella entering the
theatre, only it wasn't the same at all.

When I came home that afternoon, Mr. Simpson and
Mrs. Jackson were sitting at our kitchen table with my

mother and father. Ronnie and Ryan sat on the floor near
the fridge, eating doughnuts. Mrs. Jackson had Sam on
her lap. She was crying. Dad was talking quietly to Mr.
Simpson. I suppose he was giving advice; I can see now
he'd probably been appealed to as an older man. At the
time I couldn't take it all in.

"That Stella's walked out on them," my mother said,
as I came in the door." And if she ever gets to see these
poor little tykes again, it'll be far too soon."

As far as I know, she never did. She tried once, I think.
About a month after she left, she came back one afternoon. We were having dinner when we heard her
screaming upstairs, though we couldn't hear what she
said. Mr. Simpson's voice was there, too, running on and
on beneath hers, steady and dark like the sound of the
furnace in the basement. Then more screaming and the
clatter of Stella's heels on the stairs and the front door
slamming. I got away to the door before my mother could
stop me, but Stella was already in the taxi. There was
someone beside her, a blond man, and maybe he said
something because she turned, just as the taxi pulled
away and I saw her lean towards the window, her mouth
open. I started down the steps, but there wasn't time for
anything. The taxi took off just as my mother came to the
door.

"Inside this minute, young lady. It's none of your
business."

She stood there, holding the door for me, waiting.
Upstairs I could hear Ronnie and Ryan yelling their
heads off and Mr. Simpson saying, "Now, now, boys . . .
now, now, it's all right." His voice was smooth and
patient, like chocolate syrup and him just pouring it on
until he'd coated everything. I hated him and I hated my

mother. I hated them and I blamed them. For everything. For Stella's going off in the taxi and for Ryan's and Ronnie's bawling, which never let up, and for my having to obey my mother and follow her into the house. I guess I'd say now that I had to. To make sense at all, the whole thing had to be somebody's fault.

I started this by telling you how Stella tossed those scarves down with both hands, as if she were showering on me everything she owned. After she left in the taxi, Mr. Simpson got a transfer to a theatre in Hamilton and my parents finally bought a new house in Alston Park. It was a brand new house; no one had lived in it but us, and that seemed to give it a feeling that was way different from the apartment, an emptiness it would take a long time to fill. It was the same kind of feeling I had when I tried to think of Stella, as if every memory of her had been cut out of my brain and I couldn't bring them back no matter how hard I tried.

The summer after we moved, I got a job at the Dairy Queen at Clearlake Park. I was in love with a boy named Fraser who worked there, and, to my surprise, he was in love with me. We'd try to get night shifts together so we could neck between customers in the back room. My body felt the way the cicadas sounded in the trees outside, all buzzy and hot while I served up ice-cream cones and double malt blizzards.

I thought this was something visible, as if the hum I felt inside came out through my skin. I was still enough of a child to think I was transparent, especially to my mother, and this made me more sullen than ever around her. More *unwilling,* I guess, which, of course, made her angry or despairing, depending on the situation. "Selfish" was the word she had for me that summer, though we both knew that wasn't what she meant at all.

This night I was coming home from work really late. Fraser and I had gone down to the lake after our shift. My dad was away, he'd taken Carl on a camping trip, but I knew my mother would be waiting up. I had my story ready about how we'd had a lot of cleaning up to do, but I was scared my mouth wouldn't co-operate. It felt swollen and zingy. My whole body felt that way, as if my blood were pushing against my skin in all the places Fraser had touched me, making them incandescent, like the glow between my fingers when I held a flashlight to the palm of my hand.

I came in the side door, where there was a little landing between the steps that led into the basement and the three up to the kitchen door. I could hear voices in the kitchen. One of my mother's friends, I couldn't tell who, all her friends seemed the same to me. I knew my mother wouldn't say anything to me in front of whoever it was, but I also knew she'd expect me to be polite, to remember this lady's name and answer her dumb questions about my job. I wasn't up to it. I could feel my face taking on the closed, glum expression my mother particularly hated.

They hadn't heard me, although the kitchen door was halfway open, enough for a bit of light to shine on me as I stood there, holding the outside door open behind me. I had a trick of letting it close inch by inch so that my mother couldn't hear the click of the latch. I kept it open a crack, giving myself a few minutes before I had to go on up the steps.

"Forty-eight hours like that, forty-eight hours. They just left me there. An intern came in twice during that whole time. Twice . . . and nothing for the pain, nothing . . ."

It took me a minute to recognize my mother's voice. Something about it gave me the creeps, something I'd never heard before.

"They pulled her out with forceps, it was awful, her head all squashed and she was as blue as that cup, I swear. I thought she was dead, there was so much blood I . . ."

It was more like a smell than a sound, really, her voice. It took my breath away. It made me feel the way I felt when I saw her squatting in the bathtub every morning. I could see her with her bum stuck out and her knees half-bent, I could see the fine white lines that webbed the skin on her buttocks and thighs and the thick, wet curl of her pubic hair and how small it was, really, that place between her legs.

They pulled her out with forceps.

It made me feel queasy, though I didn't quite know what forceps were. Woozy, I mean. Like at the dentist. Something precise and shiny the dentist would use to pull a tooth, the wet, snapping sound as the root gave, the spongy, salty hole he'd stuff with cotton later. I didn't want that to have anything to do with me inside my mother's body. I didn't want her to carry on like this, her voice full of tears and snot, about something that happened my whole lifetime ago, as if it were still happening.

And that's when I thought of Stella for the first time since she'd left. I know it sounds crazy, what with my mother crying and me outside the door listening, my knees trembling. But all of a sudden, there she was, inside my head. Stella. Her smoky, spicy scent was so strong that, for a moment, I thought she really was there, upstairs, in our kitchen. I could even see her at the table with my mother, and me there, too, somehow, sitting between them, listening.

For a moment, anything was possible. But then I saw the back of her head in a taxi and that of a blond man, I didn't know who. Would never know. I saw the taxi pulling away and me standing there useless. Helpless — just like I felt out there on the steps, holding my breath, listening to my mother.

And then, of course, the full power of their stubbornness and their mystery struck me. Stella's and my mother's. It was all around me and, at the same time, in me, somehow, like the deposits of light and heat and high-pitched whirring sounds that Fraser's hands had left in my body. It was like I just discovered something, and, at the same time, discovered that I'd known it all along, so that it started to dawn on me that I could never stop knowing it again. About the most unlikely people. My brother Carl, for instance, or people I hadn't even met. Fraser, even.

At the time, though, all this just sort of flickered through my mind, like a glimpse or a word I didn't quite get. I couldn't stand there all night, eavesdropping on my mother. I had to let the door swing in and pretend I'd just got home. I had to throw the bag with my uniform in it down the basement stairs in the general direction of the washer and take off my shoes on the mat.

Upstairs I could hear my mother push her chair back, run the tap in the kitchen sink. She must have given her eyes a quick splash with cold water and tried to dry her

face on the tea towel. It was still in her hand when I
came in, a few droplets caught in her hair as she turned
towards me, her selfish, difficult daughter, who could
never, ever let on.

IF THIS IS LOVE

I

Lee Stewart likes to remember the summer of 1974, when she was pregnant with Allison, as the hottest summer of her life. "The hottest summer on record" is what she's saying these days, actually. Anyone who checked the records would find out differently, of course, but who would? Such records, as we all know, are irrelevant. Like statistics and social theory, they have little to do with a person's real life. The history that matters is the history we can use.

Daniel, Lee's first, had been born in March, out of a dreamy, snowbound winter in a farmhouse she and Blake had sublet from some friends who'd gone to

Europe. The deal was they got the place for next to nothing since Blake was finishing off the attic. Lee sat by the woodstove all day drinking coffee and reading her way through the small, haphazard collection of books at the local library. So small and haphazard, in fact, that she chose them by colour, depending on her mood – red when she was feeling bright and intellectual, green when she wanted something witty, blue near the end of her term when she was more contemplative. At least that's how she remembers it, just as she remembers that it seemed to work.

But for Allison it was summer, July arriving overnight, as it always does in Southern Ontario, taking over the city with the same stunning thoroughness that the baby took over her body. Every room in her house, every cell in her brain seemed swollen with it. She managed to drag one lawn chair out of the garage and lower herself into it, but that was about all. It seemed miles from there to the tap at the side of the house where she turned on the sprinkler for Daniel, her movements slow and clumsy as a waterlogged swimmer's. More miles still to the kitchen for Kool-Aid. The thought of two months of this began to defeat her in the damp, mouldy way that the piles of laundry did, or the sight of mildew spreading near the shower head where the tiles had come loose.

Thursday and Friday she spent just sitting there in the backyard staring, saving her strength. By Saturday she had a plan.

She was up and dressed by eight and out of the house by 8:30 A.M., leaving Daniel with Blake. She wanted to be at the mall when the stores opened and she was. Canadian Tire first for a large, three-tiered, plastic wading pool, then to Sears for two maternity bathing suits (one green, one black), several pairs of boys' trunks and one of those plastic pail-and-shovel sets that were right there, on sale, in the next bin. At the record store she splurged on five albums, including Dylan's latest, *Planet Waves*. At the beer store on the way home she picked up several cases of O'Keefe OV and at the Discount Dairy, two tubs of ice cream (one strawberry, one chocolate ripple) and their entire supply (144) of orange popsicles.

And that was it. That was all she did that summer. What she remembers of the rest of it is cool water sloshing over her belly as she sprawls in the pool drinking cold beer and eating popsicles, Daniel paddling beside her or eating an ice-cream cone on his swing under the trees. Around them, the grass turns brown, the garden wilts, the tar on the driveway melts. Lee doesn't care. She sets up the stereo on the back porch and turns it on full blast. *Planet Waves* over and over again. Sometimes she hauls herself out of the pool to push Daniel on his swing in time to "Forever Young" or "You Angel You" while, in its time, too, the baby turns and swims and waits.

A very gentle time, Lee thinks now, when she turns, as she does occasionally, and sees herself there, with Daniel, suspended in that clear, golden light. Gentle, in spite of the heat. Lee likes the way she looks in her green bathing suit, the shine of it on her great round belly and breasts, her hair piled carelessly on top of her head, curling in fine, blonde tendrils around her face. She likes Daniel's plump, gritty knees and the precision of the tan-and-dirt line around his face, just at the edges of his sun-whitened hair. Sure, she knows that's she's making it into one of those posters they had then, where pregnant women walk through meadows or along beaches under words like "You are a child of the universe," but she likes it that way. She survived.

II

On August 29 it rained all day and Daniel managed to smear peanut butter all over *Planet Waves* during the five minutes Lee was talking to her sister Jill on the phone. The next day the pool sprang a leak and on August 31, at 2:30 A.M., Allison was born. Born and nearly died, a dozen times over the next two years. Two years that seem like twenty to Lee, even now, blurred and swollen by the panic into which every other detail has collapsed – as the ordinary noise and movement of the city streets collapsed into the corridor of silence the ambulance made on the way to Emergency, the tight, tentative rasp of the child's breath, the terrible retching as she vomited again and again. Her own voice, separate, almost distant, screaming, "Don't die, Allison. Oh, god, don't, don't die."

Food allergies, they discovered finally. Minute amounts of food, even in Lee's milk, could kill. Tomatoes. Nuts, especially. A minor alteration in her diet, some medication, and Allison bloomed. Lanky and fine-boned like her mother, with her father's startling combination of blond hair and brown eyes. Healthy as hell, but a picky eater, of course, though it drives Lee crazy sometimes. Sometimes, even now, she has to grip the edge of the table to keep from shaking the kid silly. Especially when she gets that mewling, persnickety look on her face just before she spits something back on her plate.

"For godssake, Allison! I made those muffins myself. There are no nuts in them."

"I don't care. They make my throat itch. I'm not eating them."

"Allison! What do you think you're trying to pull here?"

"Nothing, I just don't want muffins. Why can't you just make toast?"

Really, it drives Lee crazy sometimes. The irritable fussiness of people with allergies. As if the world's to blame for letting peanuts and ragweed grow, cats flourish. Understandable maybe, but even so.

III

Unexpectedly, on the car radio, when they are driving back from Blake's mother's, late, the kids asleep in the back seat. Bob Dylan, singing "Forever Young."

Eight years ago this summer, Lee thinks, but what she can feel is the heat, the tickle of sweat along her hairline and the prick of sharp, dry grass on her bare feet as she gives Daniel one more push . . .

"Hey, I know that song!" Allison's voice from the back seat is almost a surprise, almost an intrusion. "Remember, Mom? You used to play it for me when I was sick all those times in the hospital."

"Allison, you've got it mixed up, honey. I don't remember ever playing that song for you. You must have heard it somewhere else."

"No, it was you. In the hospital. I know it was you."

"I don't think so, Al. And besides, you were just a baby when you were in the hospital."

"I know I'm right. *You* just don't remember."

Stubborn, fussy Allison. Once she gets an idea in her head . . . Lee feels the wearying, familiar anger start to fill her, the old push-pull, something in her stubborn as Allison, stubborn as pregnancy itself.

"But Allison – "

"*I* remember it" – Danny's voice now, cracked with sleep. His coming in brings back something from Lee's own childhood. Driving home from her grandparents' like this, talking quietly with her mother, her father joining in and then her sister's voice, sharp and surprising.

"Another country heard from," her mother used to say, as each one spoke.

And it was like that, somehow. Another country.

". . . on that record you used to have. Remember, Mom?"

"But that was before Allison was born, Dan. When I used to push you in the swing that summer, remember, when we had the pool."

"I was there, too!"

"Allison, you fluff-brain! You heard what Mom said; you weren't even born."

"I don't care. I remember it. It's my favourite song."

"Yeah, sure. Next you're gonna tell us you heard it in the womb."

"That's enough, Dan."

"Well, you never know," Blake's voice, suddenly, half-joking, half-thoughtful, too. "Anything is possible."

Another country heard from.

"Oh, Blake, really. Now, we'll never hear the end of it."
And, of course, they won't.

IV

"Allison, what on earth are you doing?" Lee comes in
one Saturday afternoon to find her daughter curled up on
the floor against one of the stereo speakers.

"I'm just listening to this. It's my own record. I bought
it with my own money."

"You really like it that much, eh?" Lee tries to keep her
voice easy, but she can already feel the tightening in her
throat.

"Yes. I told you. It's my favourite song. It makes me
feel safe." Allison pauses for a minute. She gets this look;
Lee can't decide whether to call it stubborn or sly, but
she recognizes it. "Especially when you and Dad are
fighting," she says, determinedly.

"Fighting? Is that what you think we're doing?" Lee
can hear herself, can hear the aggressive patience of the
reasonable parent, but she can't help it.

"Well, aren't you?"

"I wouldn't call it fighting, exactly."

"I know, I know. *You* call it *discussing*. But it sounds
like fighting to me."

Last night, at the kitchen table, after the kids had gone
to bed, Lee can see Blake leaning towards her. ("But why,
Lee, why? I just don't understand. Surely if we talk about
it . . . I can change, really. Lee . . . ") She can see the look
on his face; that open, almost vulnerable expression that

she used to love and can't stand any longer. ("No you can't! That's the whole goddamn point. You *can't* change.")

Or won't. She doesn't know anymore.

She turns to the window and sees him, squatting on the flat roof of the garage with Daniel, showing him how to nail down the supports for the backboard for his basketball hoop. The two of them squat in exactly the same position, blond and solid against the sky. Blake is going over the procedure step by step, amiable, patient as always, his tone (though Lee can't hear it, she knows) that of a man who cannot imagine that others do not share his passion for detail, his –

"Allison! Jesus! That's the third goddamn time you've played that!" Again, it seems to Lee that her voice comes from someone else, startling her as much as it does Allison, the child's face filling with hurt and surprise.

"Please, honey. I didn't mean to yell. Just turn it down, eh? Or use the headphones."

But it's too late, of course. Even though Allison obeys immediately. Plugs in the headphones and slips them on, turning her back on Lee, swaying to her song. Even though Lee heads for the kitchen to start supper. She can hear it still, that stupid song, on and on in her head, like the image of her daughter's strong, defiant back leaning into it.

V

"But, Mom, what do you r*eally* think? *Could* I have heard it, inside somehow?"

Four years later, Allison's insistence that she re-members, from the womb, a Bob Dylan album hardly anyone else even listens to is something of a family joke, even for her. By this time, her parents have had what their friends and they themselves call "an amicable divorce." No legal wrangling, no holding the children hostage to unfinished business, as so many of us do. Lee and Blake have been decent, even kind. They have read that this sort of attitude makes it easier for children to accept divorce and they believe it. Who wouldn't? Though what our children decide to make of what we do for them (assuming it really is for them) is anybody's guess.

So if Allison likes to believe that she remembers a song she heard only in an earlier existence – before her life was threatened by allergies or complicated by her parents' divorce – who knows? She also likes the scary and the weird horror movies Lee can't even watch with the lights on.

Tonight is Hallowe'en. Allison is going to the party at the school as a goblin. She's dyed her hair green, using hair gel and food colouring and is sitting in the kitchen with Lee, waiting for it to dry. Her costume, which she made herself, is hidden under her bathrobe, only to be revealed when Lee's painted her face.

"Could I have, Mom?"

"I don't know, Al." Lee is opening a box of grease-paints, peeling the foil back from the sticks. She'd really rather not go over this again, but she also knows Allison won't be put off. So she tries. "I read an article the other day about some experiment that shows babies are affected by sounds outside the womb, but one specific album seems a little much to me. Here, hold still now."

She starts spreading basic white over Allison's face, ears and neck.

"Diana plays music for her baby all the time," Allison counters. "Classical music. Last weekend, she went around at Grandma's with the earphones of her Walkman on her belly."

Diana. Blake's sister. It figures.

Goblin eyes, now. Outlined in black, filled in with shimmery blue-green. A little white in there will make them look more prominent, bulging with mischief. Or malice.

Allison, looking out at her, waiting for an answer.

"What does your dad say?" Dark green along the sides of the nose and then a lighter, almost yellowy gold along the top. A splash of gold glitter on the tip. Pixieish.

Allison giggles. "He says maybe that's why I'm such a goofball. From listening to one song all the time and bouncing around inside you while you danced."

"Danced?" Lee is genuinely puzzled, but Allison looks up at her, still giggling, as if she's teasing.

"Yeah, *you* know! How you moved the table in the dining room and danced around with Daniel.

For a minute there, Lee can see it, too. She's wearing some loose, long Indian-print thing, her hair loose, too, not all pinned up on her head. She can feel the cool, bare floor under her bare feet, the weight of Daniel in her arms, his feet kicking softly against the sides of her belly, the baby . . .

"I don't remember any dancing, hon. It was too hot. We were outside all summer. It was the hottest summer on record."

"Daddy said it rained."

"Jesus, Allison, sit still." Lee is trying to get the dark green even, along the jawline and the neck, trying to make it look like scales or warty skin. And she really wants to let this whole conversation drop. She's sick of it.

"I don't remember it raining," she says firmly, "and I don't remember dancing, but I did play the record, okay? I played it over and over again. Maybe you did hear it somehow. I just don't think it's possible for you to remember . . . "

"Daddy says that anything is possible."

"I don . . . "

Let it drop, Lee. Let it drop.

"Well, maybe it is." Gold glitter on the cheekbones, hair. Just a touch of gold on the eyelids. There.

"Okay, I think that's it."

Allison jumps off her chair and starts upstairs. "I'm gonna take my bathrobe off. You light the jack-o'-lantern. No peeking. And remember, Danny's gotta take a picture for Dad!"

"Right, boss," Lee answers, but laughing, trying to do it easily.

VI

Sometimes, though, her anger takes her by surprise, right there, ready to bubble to the surface anytime, like those rashes Allison used to get. Before Lee knew what caused them, they seemed to come for no reason, pure malevolence, wilful and implacable, every inch of her baby's smooth, perfect skin bursting with furious, red welts, her rib cage heaving, alarmingly, as if her insides were about to tear through, her tiny face unrecognizable.

An "amicable divorce." What did it mean, really? Saying they were still friends, Blake coming in for his ritual cup of coffee when he picks up the kids. She can see them all sitting there while he drinks it, her trying to make conversation, the kids looking on. What good does it do, finally? What good does it do anyone?

Sometimes, when she calls Blake these days, there's a funny pause after she says hello, when she realizes she has to say, "It's me, Lee." As if he weren't sure. As if her voice had changed somehow. Sometimes she feels the urge to start shouting, crazily, the way some people do when they're talking to someone from another country, someone they think doesn't understand English.

Sometimes she's just not sure how much longer she can keep this up. Or whether she even wants to.

VII

"Wow, Allison!" Even Daniel, summoned from in front of the TV, is impressed. Lee's glad he's there, clapping and whistling, checking the camera for film. She wants to cry, throw her arms around Allison, say something motherish and corny. "My beautiful elfin child."

And she *is* elfin, dammit. The way she's taken a green leotard and stitched on patches cut from a blue satin evening dress she got at the Thrift Shop, layering them like bright scales along her arms, chest and back. One shoulder's stuffed with a small pillow, so that her slight frame twists grotesquely, her hands (turquoise gloves, starched stiff) extending like claws, her hair snaking green and stringy around her face.

And her face! Did I really do that? Lee wonders. Certainly no human child, this, not with that nose, that skin that seems to ripple in the light from the jack-o'-lantern, the eyes bright slits in which Lee can imagine she sees small, independent flames already flickering.

"Ugh, Allison, this is creepy. We've really outdone ourselves."

But Allison is already turning to the hallway for her coat. "Let's go! It's after nine."

Outside, the street's nearly empty; the last of the younger trick-or-treaters knocked at their door over an hour ago. They pick up Allison's friends, Laura and Elaine, now a witch and a mummy, and drive to the school where other cars are lined up, spilling out white clouds of exhaust (like those seed pods in *Invasion of the Body Snatchers*, Lee thinks) from which step ghouls and space creatures, gypsies, frogs, a tin soldier.

"Laura, your mom's picking you guys up, right?"

"Yup, eleven o'clock for sure."

"See ya, Mom." Allison already has her coat off, dancing with excitement. Lee waves and pulls away, but there's a moment when she catches her in the rearview mirror, half off the ground, a flying thing, will-o'-the-wisp. Suddenly, she's frightened. She doesn't know why, but frightened enough to brake slightly, consider going back before the three creatures link arms and turn to where the double doors of the school swing open, push them inside.

VIII

When the phone rings, Lee and Daniel are half asleep in front of the TV. Lee turns down the volume and glances at her watch before she answers. Ten-forty-five. It's probably Laura's mom, with car trouble. Damn, she'll have to go out again.

"Hello."

"Mrs. Reynolds?"

Mrs. Reynolds? Oh, yes. "Well, I go by Stewart, actually I . . . "

"Allison Reynolds' mother?"

Allison. Allison!

"Yes, what's . . . "

"No need for alarm, Mrs. Reynolds. It's Dr. Baker at Hotel Dieu Emergency. We have your daughter here. It seems she got into some nuts at her school party and she's having a mild allergic reaction, but she'll be fine. Could you come and get her?"

Immediate itching and swelling of the throat, wheezing and congestion . . . vomiting . . . in severe cases . . . anaphylactic shock . . . fifteen to thirty minutes . . .

On the TV some local businessman dressed as Dracula is doing his own ad. The undead as used-car salesman. Lee snaps it off.

"Daniel, wake up! We gotta go! Something's happened to Allison!"

She is in the car, revving the engine frantically, before he stumbles out, climbs in beside her, white and small.

"Wha . . . "

"Allison's at Emergency. She's eaten some nuts."

Allison. She hasn't had a reaction since she was five. She *knows*. She always asks, at least twice. Fussy, fussy Allison.

"C'mon Allison, for Pete's sake, just try it, at least! I've read the label. See! No nuts . . . "

"I don't care! It itches my throat."

Goddammit, Allison! What do you think you're pulling?

IX

At Emergency, there's a jack-o'-lantern on the admitting desk; a witch on a broomstick sails over the waiting room. A short, soft-faced man comes towards her, carrying a clipboard.

"Mrs. Reynolds? Hi, I'm Dr. Baker. I spoke with you on the phone. Are you aware that your daughter is allergic to nuts?"

"Of course I am! She hasn't had a reaction since she was five. She's always very careful."

"Yes, of course. But accidents do happen."

Dr. Baker looks to be about Daniel's age. He's definitely shorter. *Accidents do happen.* Lee wants to pat him on the head as she pushes past him.

"Where is she now?"

Dr. Baker puts his hand out as if to hold her back. "Just down the hall, Mrs. Reynolds. I've notified your regular doctor, Dr. Bryson. Does Allison have an allergist?"

"Of course. Dr. Wyman. Could I just see her now, please?"

"I suggest you take her to Dr. Wyman on Monday, Mrs. Reynolds; it might be wise for Allison to carry an adrenaline kit at all times."

But Lee has already started down the corridor. Dr. Baker puts down his clipboard and follows, half-running, so that by the time they reach the first room he's caught up and is leading the way. Lee can feel Daniel just behind her . . .

"Right in here, Mrs. Reynolds."

Later, Lee will learn that Allison *did* ask about the cookies. And on Monday the allergist will say: Yes, such incidents are slightly more common at this age. Practical jokes on the part of peers, usually, not realizing how serious it really is. Though sometimes the child herself, strangely enough, will eat something she knows she shouldn't. Testing her limits, perhaps. Adolescent bravado. You know how kids this age think they're immortal. Or maybe just the imp of the perverse. Who can say?

Later tonight, Lee will call Blake and when Allison wakes in the morning, feeling woozy from the drugs, but fine, he will be there. Blake and Lee will stand at the door of Allison's room, holding hands, briefly, as people do when they realize, if only for the moment, that what holds them together for good and carries them into the future is not dependant on their decency or even their desire to be kind. Rejects all their fine plans, in fact, as fiercely as the body rejects our attempts to make it more or less than simply what it is.

But, for now, there is only the door swinging open and Allison there on the bed, still in her goblin costume, her green face smeared with tears and mucus, the familiar red welts already rising under the makeup. Stubborn, fussy Allison who possibly does remember songs she heard in the womb as fiercely as Lee remembers that heat and how she survived it, who cares how or why.

Allison, now. Ugly and wonderful, like someone returned from the dead. Which, of course, she is. So that even Dr. Baker seems to hesitate, and, behind her, Lee hears Daniel say for the second time that night:

"Wow! Allison!"

FOR PUZZLED IN WISCONSIN

Dear Allie: My husband has an intricate tattoo on his chest. I am very fond of it, and don't want to see it go with him when he dies.

I'm wondering if there is a way to have it taken off and preserved somehow at the time of his passing. Is this against the law? If not, who would look after this sort of thing, should it be possible: a taxidermist, the funeral director, or someone else?

My husband enjoys the best of health now, but I'd like to know what your answer is so that I can prepare myself.

– Puzzled in Wisconsin

My daughter reads me your letter, laughing.

"Do you believe this?" she says, in the voice she has for the tabloids at the checkout at Loblaws. "Baby Born Repeating Message from Aliens!" "I Saw My Husband Snatched by a Mermaid."

"Do you believe this!" Not a question, of course, since for her the answer is obvious.

After she goes off to do her homework, I pick up the paper and read your letter through again, two or three times, until I can see you there at your kitchen table writing it. Beside you is a coffee mug and a pack of Player's Light. The mug says I ❤ my mutt and there's a picture on it of a dog like the one that's lying by the door watching you.

You're just about due for a perm and a rinse. Your hair's showing grey at the roots, greyer than mine, I think, but fine like mine and straggly. Faded blonde, like your skin, which is dry and washed-out looking under your blush and your blue eye shadow.

When your husband gets off work tonight – he's on afternoons this week – the letter will be in your purse, which is on the sideboard in the dining room. I can see you in the living room with your bathrobe on, watching "Johnny Carson." Your husband usually brings home a pizza or some Chinese and you both have a couple of beers. Then he'll start sucking on your earlobe or tickling your breasts. It's fun, not having to worry anymore about the kids hearing. Your baby, Tommy, moved out on his own three months ago.

At this point, your husband pulls his T-shirt off. You like to run your tongue over his tattoo. Sometimes, that's all you do. Sometimes, that's just for starters.

Dear Puzzled: Ask the funeral director when the time comes. He (or she) will be able to answer your questions. In the meantime, perhaps someone who knows will see this and let me know if anything of the sort has been done before, and, if so, how they handled it.

I, too, am puzzled.

Well, she didn't exactly bust her ass trying to find an answer, did she? *I, too, am puzzled.* When you read that out loud it sounds kind of snotty, as if she thinks this can't be serious. *When the time comes . . .* Oh, brilliant. When the time comes you'll have a million other things on your mind. The boys'll make fun of you, the undertaker will pat you on the arm and say: "There, there, you're just upset." It gets you upset, all right, just thinking about it.

Your husband just thinks you're weird. "But what the hell," he says, "go ahead if you want to. They're already gonna take my eyes and my liver. Might as well have my tattoo, too."

He doesn't know about the letter, of course. He never reads "Dear Allie." "They just make that shit up," he says, "to sell papers."

The summer I was eighteen, I worked as a waitress at the Bangor Lodge in Muskoka. Most of the other waitresses were girls like me, just finished high school, earning money for university in the fall, but the cooking staff were all local, from Bracebridge or Huntsville. They worked there every summer and on into the off-season after the rest of us left. Most of them were women my mother's age, except for the girl who did the salads and the bread baskets and stuff.

Gwen MacIntyre. She was my age, though she looked older. Short and busty with thick black hair and huge violet eyes. Like Liz Taylor, of course, and she emphasized that, piling her hair up in thick curls and wearing lots of dark eyeliner. On her it was okay, too. She really was beautiful, just as Liz herself *was* beautiful, temporarily, but perfectly, before she got all bloated and silly.

Usually the waitresses didn't hang around much with the kitchen staff, but Gwen and I soon found we had something in common. Our boyfriends both worked in Toronto. Gwen's boyfriend, Chuck, was a welder; my boyfriend, Jeff, was working at a paint factory for the summer.

"I suppose he's comin' up on the weekend, eh?" Gwen asked, though she didn't really put it as a question. It was just sort of assumed. She'd already told me that Chuck came up every Saturday.

"Probably not, actually." I tried to sound casual, but I felt, somehow, apologetic. "He doesn't have a car."

"Well, why didn't you say so? He can drive up with Chuck and we can do something together. It'll be great."

That night, Gwen phoned Chuck to tell him the plan.

"He'll pay half the gas," she said, which is what we'd agreed she'd say, "and he can get over to your place, easy. All you have to do is call him up and introduce yourself. Anna's gonna call him first, right after I hang up. She's really nice, honey. It'll be great. See you Saturday. Bye, hon."

She always called him "honey" or "hon." He called her "babe." I couldn't imagine Jeff calling me anything.

"Jesus, I don't even know the guy," he kept saying. "Why didn't you call me first."

"If you don't want to come," I said after a few minutes of this, "don't bother." And I hung up, hard.

We were using the phone in the little office just off the kitchen where the cook made up the orders and paid the delivery men. You had to reverse the charges. There'd been a minute at the start when I thought Jeff wasn't going to accept and, now that I'd hung up, I realized he couldn't call me back. Even if he bothered to find out, the only number listed for the lodge was the front desk. They didn't take personal calls for staff.

Gwen was in the kitchen putting the last of the dishes in the dishwasher, but she didn't try to hide the fact that she was listening. As soon as I banged the phone down, she came to the door with a coffee and my cigarettes.

"Don't worry," she said, "he'll show up."

As it turned out, she was right. Jeff said he thought Chuck was a bit of an asshole, but he could stand it, so the summer was set. They both had to work Saturdays and, what with holiday traffic and all, they usually didn't get to the lodge before 9:30 or 10:00 P.M. By that time, we'd be pretty well finished. If I had a late table, Gwen'd help me set up for breakfast, though she wasn't supposed to.

Chuck had an old Ford pickup that his father had sold him for a dollar when he started working in Toronto. The passenger door was so rusted he'd had to weld it shut, so everyone piled in from the driver's side. By half past ten, we'd be heading out to a spot he knew about along the lake where there was a bit of a beach and no other cottages. We'd build a fire and sit around drinking beer and listening to Jeff's radio. After an hour or so, Chuck'd grab Gwen and say, "C'mon, babe, come and say hello to your old man," and they'd move off a ways into the little woods while Jeff and I stretched out by the fire.

The air was always hot and close and still. You could hear everything. Especially Chuck.

"Oh, babe!" he'd say. "Oh, babe!" And then louder and louder. "Oh, babe, oh, Gwennie, oh-h, oh-h, babe!" Then silence. Then it would start again.

Later, driving back to the lodge, I'd try to fit Chuck's face – which was broad and fair and sort of *eager*, I guess, but in the way a kid's face is eager, one front tooth chipped, the other missing – to the sounds I heard in the woods, but I never could. It was like it never happened. Jeff never even let on, but one night, just as he came inside me, he started whining in this forced, stupid whisper: "Oh, babe, oh, babe." I pushed him away and tried to stand up.

"Hey" – he held me – "c'mon. I was only fooling."

"Yeah, I know." I wanted to punch him, to hurt him in some way I knew I never could. I don't know why.

Jeff and I always used a safe, of course, but I knew for a fact, because she told me, that Gwen and Chuck never did. I wasn't surprised. There'd been lots of Gwens at my high school. I knew exactly what would happen.

By the end of August, Gwen was pregnant. Chuck was ecstatic. He even brought a bottle of champagne up the next weekend. He'd already found a bigger apartment. They planned to get married on the Labour Day weekend, though Gwen would go on working at the lodge until it closed in October. They could use the extra money.

Jeff and I used to talk about getting married, too, but it was just talk. He was going to Queen's, to med school, in the fall and he kept saying he wanted me to come there instead of going to Western. He talked about how a small apartment would be cheaper than residence.

Knowing what I know now, this would have meant my getting a part-time job to help with expenses, failing courses, getting pregnant and then finding out five years down the road that Jeff was in love with some night nurse and wanted a divorce. At the time, I just didn't like the way he kept kissing the back of my neck when I tried to talk about something I'd read or even about one of my customers.

"Is this what you really want to do?" I asked Gwen once.

She looked as if she thought I must be joking. "Of course. Don't you?"

That was all she said. I thought it was because she was too stupid to want anything else. I guess I saw her as a victim of her own life, forced into it because she hadn't been smart enough to plan ahead. I never even considered then that she might see me in the same light.

Peter, the man I *did* marry, sixteen years ago, is an archivist at the university. When our daughter read him your letter, he laughed with her, but for different reasons. He can believe it all right, some people are probably like that, he just doesn't think it has anything to do with him. When they laugh, both Peter and our daughter, Jennifer, dip their heads slightly to the side at precisely the same angle, mouths wide open, showing the same even teeth.

That night in bed, I ask Peter, "Is there anything like that of mine you'd want to save?"

"Like what?"

"You know, that "Dear Allie" letter Jennifer read about the tattoo."

"Of course not; I'd never even think of it."

"Well, think about it now. *If* you were going to do something like that, what would you want? Some of my stretch marks? The mole on my left breast?"

"I can't imagine it, Anna. Really, this is silly."

He lies flat on his back, his hands at his sides, his eyes closed, his face set in the pained expression he wears for conversations like this – "What if's" speculations. When Jennifer and I sit in a restaurant making up stories about the people around us, he closes his eyes, just as he's doing now.

"Tightass. You never even try."

"I just can't, Anna. You know that. I don't know what you want me to do."

"I don't, either." I try to make it light, nonchalant. "Night." I kiss him lightly as I reach across him to turn off the lamp, then roll over as if to sleep. I don't want him to think I'm angry, it's just a silly game, after all.

I don't even want to *be* angry, dammit. It's not like he isn't imaginative. He is – about gifts, for example, and vacations. I don't think this other is something he can do anything about, and why should he? Once I asked him if he ever made up stories about the material at the archives, the people whose bits and pieces he sorts and labels.

"Of course not, Anna. I'd never get any work done."

And I can see what he means. His job is to organize the known world, after all. It's up to someone else to explore the rest. Why should I hold it against him?

But I do. Just because I understand doesn't mean it doesn't poke at me, niggling and sore, like the pea under all those mattresses in the fairy story.

After a few minutes, I get up and slip on my bathrobe. Peter, who can sleep through anything, doesn't move, even his breathing stays slow and regular.

Downstairs, the house has that smooth, mirror-like quality that always makes me feel like a figure in someone else's dream. I grab a glass and the bourbon and go out on the deck at the back. It's hot tonight. All the houses are open, relaxed, letting go of their secrets. A toilet flushes, a baby cries, a man's voice coaxes a cat inside. "Susie, c'mon now, Susie, come and see Daddy." It's not very often that I sit here, late like this, with my feet on the railing, drinking bourbon. I wish I had a cigarette. I wish I could stay up all night, drinking and smoking.

The first time I ever drank bourbon was with Gwen and Chuck and Jeff at Chuck's parents' house. The boys had come up one Saturday, as usual, but just as they pulled in, it started to rain, hard. We didn't know what to do.

"Hop in," Chuck said. "We'll go see my folks. They won't mind."

Chuck's parents, Roy and Joan, were sitting at the kitchen table when we came up to the back porch. Roy was an older version of Chuck with the same eager face, even the missing tooth. He was wearing a baggy pair of Bermuda shorts and a green T-shirt with ART'S ESSO in black across the chest. Joan was wearing shorts, too, white, with a white halter top and a man's plaid flannel shirt, open, over the whole thing. Her hair, which was dark brown (obviously, but gloriously dyed), was teased and piled into a high beehive. On her feet she had gold, high-heeled slippers.

They both jumped up as soon as they saw us.

"Hey there, Chuckie boy!" Roy shouted. "C'mon in outta the rain." He pulled chairs up around the table, while Joan brought over glasses and a forty-ouncer of bourbon.

"You're workin' with Gwen at the lodge then," she said, handing me a drink and holding out her pack of cigarettes.

"Yeah, in the dining room, though. I'm a waitress."

"Tips good?"

"Yeah, I guess so. I get about one hundred dollars a week."

"Shit!" Joan exhaled smoke sharply. "You hear that Roy? One hundred lousy bucks a week in tips at Bangor. Cheapskates. What you don't have to put up with, eh?"

She laughed, but even her laugh had an edge to it, angry, as if she were personally involved.

I took another sip of my bourbon. I'd never drunk liquor straight before. I was beginning to like the way it stung my tongue, burned my whole mouth frozen all the way down. One hundred a week in tips had seemed like a lot to me, but now I could see what Joan meant. I thought about how people's voices sounded when they gave their order, how they always stopped talking to each other when I came up to the table.

We sat around drinking and smoking for what seemed like hours. Food kept appearing. Some doughnuts Joan had made fresh that morning, salami and cheese, crackers, homemade pickles.

All of a sudden Roy leaned back in his chair and pulled his T-shirt up almost to his neck.

"What do ya think of this baby here?" he asked.

Across his middle, from his belt line to just below his left nipple was a wide, jagged, white scar. He had a lot of hair, but it hadn't grown back over the scar, which was thicker in some places than others. It glistened and bulged in the yellow kitchen light, stretched taut over his gut as if the skin couldn't take much more.

"Quite a mess, eh?" He said. "I used to be a guard at the Pen in Kingston, there. Had some trouble one night. One of the guys had a shank. Ripped me open in one swipe. Felt like he'd sliced my liver out. Next thing I know, I'm wakin' up in the hospital."

He took another swig of bourbon and lit a cigarette off the one he had going. "Turned out I lost a lot of blood, but that was about it. The guy missed every single vital organ. Can you believe it? Every single goddamn vital organ. The doctors said I was the luckiest sonofabitch they'd ever seen. I wanted to go right back as soon as the stitches were out, but Joan here, she said she couldn't take it, what with the kids and all, especially the nights. So I let 'er go. Ten years seniority, pension, the whole goddamn shot."

He let go of his shirt so that it dropped slightly and wrinkled around his gut. Nobody said anything, but it wasn't from embarrassment or shock or anything like that. It was more as if we weren't expected to.

Whenever I have told this story – and I have, many times – I always tell about Roy and the scar, of course, but it's just part of it, part of the story about that summer and about Gwen and Chuck (neither of whom I ever saw again, after the season ended, though we promised we'd visit), and about drinking bourbon all night. I tell about going out to drive back to the lodge and seeing the sky lightening over the trees and realizing that we'd been up all night, Gwen and me working all day Sunday, no sleep, hung-over and never giving it a thought. That's how the story ends when I've told it lately. How you can do it when you're young.

Not now though. So I haul myself off the deck, rinse the glass and tiptoe back upstairs. Peter doesn't wake up when I crawl into bed, but he says my name, out loud. "Anna." As if he were checking it off a list, some part of him still awake until everything's accounted for. He always does this and I always sort of like it, even though I'm still a little angry.

I'm just drifting off when I see something else. It's almost as if I'm watching a movie of the six of us in that kitchen, sitting around the table and the camera moves in all of a sudden, so that what I can see now is a close-up of Joan's hand, reaching out to Roy's bare gut, caressing it so intimately I can't believe she's doing it in front of us. And then, with the tip of her index finger, gently, very gently, she traces the scar, every turn and bulge, from

Roy's nipple to his waist, as if to show us exactly what it's like.

As if his belly were a map, almost, and the scar was this road she was pointing out, wanting us to see where he'd been. And where'd she'd been, too. After he got out of the hospital, when he spent days just sitting there, staring, and she had to keep the kids quiet, not knowing what he was going to do next, what was going to happen to them. That was part of it. And more, that we could never know.

It's just for a minute that I see this, mind you, Joan's hand on Roy's scar like that. But it's what I would want to tell you, Puzzled in Wisconsin, if I ever had the chance, or knew how.

BACK PAIN

Something is wrong. Something is wrong with her daughter, Kate. Along with everything else in her life, it seems to Barbara, everything that she can feel, building up, in the same old spot, between her shoulder blades.

"Good god, Barbara, what have you been up to?" Bev Masters moves her strong fingers determinedly up Barbara's spine to the spot where the muscles burn and scream. "Your back's a mess. You've got to let go of some of this pain."

Barbara closes her eyes and tries to relax as Bev presses deeply into the tight spot. A spasm of pain forces her breath into her throat, sends ripples of nausea through her stomach.

Let go of this pain. As if she wanted her back to hurt, for chrissake. As if this pain were something she held onto, wilfully, a wild thing with a life of its own. All she wants is a massage (a back rub is what she calls it, actually, to herself). She doesn't need Bev's line on spiritual release, not today. She's got enough to deal with without having to listen to some hippy-dippy theory about how all the pain you've ever experienced (since childhood, for godssake) is trapped inside your body until you decide to work it out.

Barbara figures the last three months will do nicely.

There's her father, for one thing. A stroke, a mild one certainly, but still. He's home from the hospital already and the physiotherapy is doing wonders, but she's been driving him back and forth to appointments – her mother, too nervous, especially in this weather – and she can feel it, now, the way she hunches over the wheel when the visibility's bad.

Then there's Marnie, the bimbo from Office Overload who's filling in while Madge is on maternity. Barbara's a secretary at Centennial Secondary School. They need three people in that office, really. Now there's just her and the human cantaloupe. Talk about a pain in the neck. Ha. Ha.

And just for the good old icing on the cake, all this happens while Norm's gone. To Norway, for godssake, for six straight months, trying to iron out some problems they're having with a new rolling process there. Norm is an engineer with Alcan, though Barbara has only the haziest notion of what he actually does.

What she's sure of is that she misses him more than she thought possible. It's not just the extra work around the house, either, though that, too, has surprised her, realizing how much he'd taken on over the years. It's the weight of it, somehow, the sheer weight of holding everything together, holding everything up, as if she were carrying the work of ten people, not just two. It reminds her of the shock she felt when Jason was born and Kate was barely two. How she'd gone through the pregnancy thinking that another one wouldn't be that much more, really. Only to find that this wasn't something you could work out that way, mathematically, a simple equation in which two kids equal twice the work. Norm's absence is like that, bigger than she'd expected it to be, as if he were more than half of what they were together, so that without him she feels less capable, less like herself. Especially now, when she knows that something's going on with Kate though she can't put her finger on it, can't . . .

"There, now, how's that feel?" Bev's voice reaches to her from a great distance, softly, her hands softer, too, it seems, warm and liquid, flowing over her back one more time. Barbara feels her muscles relax a little, if only a little.

"Ah, great, it's much better," she says, as she reaches for her clothes, and it really is.

"I wish you'd let me give you a Traeger," Bev goes on. "This type of massage can only do so much, you know, when there's so much pain there. Spiritual pain, I mean; you can't separate that . . . "

"I'll think about it," Barbara says, as she scribbles out the cheque, "but really, Bev, you did a great job already."

You and a good stiff drink, she tells herself, as she heads out to her car and drives off, stopping at the liquor store and then going straight on home, straight up to the bathroom, running the water as hot as she can stand it, testing the temperature with one hand, holding the Scotch bottle in the other.

An hour later, warm and relaxed, wrapped in an old bathrobe of Norm's, she's just put some sole in the pan and is starting to make a salad when Kate comes in.

"Hi, honey! You're just in time. I'm cooking some fish. There's loads. Want some?" Barbara tries to keep her voice light, casual, but it's hard. Having to be on . . . *on guard* all the goddamn time. With her own daughter.

At first she put it down to Kate's practically killing herself with this school production of *Pygmalion*. But then the name of Danny Saunders kept coming up. Pointedly. He's the set designer for the play. It also looks to Barbara like he's Kate's first big love. Which would be great, she tells herself. Really. Except.

Except for the way Kate *looks*, somehow. It doesn't seem right. She's pale; there are dark circles under her eyes, though what Barbara is really going by is her hair. Norm used to laugh at her, but she has always diagnosed the health of her children – both of them clear, golden blonds – by their hair, and she has seldom been wrong. Kate's, as she comes in the door, is lank and stringy. There's something sort of . . . sort of wan about it, Barbara thinks, the word surfacing inside her head suddenly, as if from a great depth, and something more with it, a line or two of poetry in the voice of Miss Simmons, her high school English teacher: *Why so pale and wan fond lover? Prithee, why so pale?*

She reaches out to smooth her daughter's hair from her cheek, a familiar gesture, her everyday way of greeting both her children.

But Kate shrugs away from her. "Do you have to keep touching me all the time," she says irritably. "You'd think I was about four years old, really."

Somewhere inside Barbara's head, a familiar alarm begins to sound. MEWS, Norm used to call it: Mothers' Early Warning System. Teasing, but respectful, too, because she could always tell. Who was coming down with chicken pox, who was skipping school, who was ... what? And what can she say?

"Sorry." Contrite. She sounds like a kid, she thinks.

"Oh, it's okay," Kate shrugs again, but her voice still has an edge to it. "It's just that I can't stand to have you fussing around when I've got so much on my mind."

"Well, eat a little salad and some sole. I'm worried about you. You don't seem to be eating anything these days." When in doubt, offer food. Breast, bottle, soother. When all else fails . . .

Kate sighs, almost good-naturedly. Almost, it seems to Barbara, as if she's humouring a troublesome child.

"Sure, Mom, but I'm okay, really. I just never knew the show was going to be this much work."

"I wish your dad were going to be here for it." Barbara slices a tomato into the salad and puts the bowl on the table.

"Yeah, well, it's not like I'm going to be in it or anything."

"Can't have a play without a stage manager. And I know you've done a lot of work on the set. I can hardly wait to see it."

"Let's just hope I don't die from lack of sleep before it's done." Kate grins, looking like herself for a minute, though not long enough to convince Barbara. She's just lifting the sole out of the pan when the phone rings. Damn.

It's her mother.

"Hi dear, am I interrupting anything?"

"Kate and I were just sitting down to dinner."

"Oh, I thought you'd be through by now. Well, I won't keep you. I was just wondering if you could pick your dad and me up at the hospital after his checkup Friday. Lana Carlson can drive us in, but she's got – "

"Sure Mom, what time?" Barbara slides the fish onto a plate with the spatula, divides it, slides half onto another plate and holds it out to Kate. For a moment, she feels the stretch between the table and the phone, between her daughter and her mother, as keenly as if the telephone wires were extensions of the cords of muscle running from one hand to the other across her back. The spot between her shoulder blades quickens.

"Could be at the out-patients entrance, off Clarence Street, oh, about a quarter past ten," her mother is saying. "We'll take the elevator down."

A quarter past ten. That means working through lunch. *And* leaving Marnie with the attendance sheets. Last time, she didn't bother to check them off against the late slips and the call-ins. *Oh, god, Mrs. Huntington, like I feel so stupid, I never even thought of that.*

You don't have to think, Marnie, it's all right there on the forms. Jesus.

"Sure, Mom, I'll be there, no problem."

"You're sure, now."

"Mom, really. Now my dinner's getting cold."

"Okay, dear. Give my love to Katie and Jas. See you Friday. Bye now."

Barbara turns to the table just as Kate stuffs the last of her salad into her mouth. She gets up as Barbara sits down.

"You're off, already? There's coffee."

"No thanks. Danny and I are going out for some. Just for an hour. Okay?"

Barbara feels Kate's lips brush the top of her head as she slips past her and on up the stairs. Two minutes later, she hears the shower running. She sighs, reaches behind her to the sideboard for the novel she's been reading, props it open on the salad bowl and takes a bite of her fish. She might as well enjoy eating alone. Norm's away, Jason's got a basketball game, Kate's in love. The universe is unfolding as it should. Good god, given the ways things have gone the last few weeks, she could certainly use a few hours of peace and quiet. No one to worry about but herself.

Except for Danny Saunders. That's it, really. What it is about that kid, she doesn't know, but Barbara does not like him. He was at Centennial for three years before he transferred to Northgrove, Kate's school, and Barbara saw him often enough in the office. Not because he was in trouble, ever, not even late, but because he was forever trying to do something complicated with his timetable, something that required the signature of the principal, Mr. Babcock. A curly-haired, almost baby-faced boy who seemed able to talk in a smooth, reasonable voice until he got what he wanted, always. He was never pushy, but he was never, well, *awkward,* either, the way most kids are when they try to wangle some kind of special deal. It drove her nuts, though she knew it didn't make any sense. Just like now, when he comes to the house. The way he keeps his arms folded across his chest, his hands stuffed in his armpits. The only sign of nervousness or discomfort he ever displays. Probably nervousness. She knows that. She still doesn't like him.

"And *you* aren't dating him." That's what Norm would say, of course. Getting right to the heart of it. *Kate's eighteen. She'll be going away to university next year. You're not in charge anymore.* All the old familiar phrases she's heard other parents use, the litany of letting go.

Kate comes back down wearing a blue sweatshirt, her hair fresh and shining after her shower. But still not right, Barbara thinks.

"Have a good time," is what she says, though. *And be careful*, to herself, like a good-luck charm.

She reaches out to touch her daughter's hair, remembers just in time, pulls her hand back, fiddles clumsily with the belt on her robe as if *that* is what she really meant to do.

"Sorry . . . " she mutters, stupidly. But Kate doesn't even notice. She's already grabbing her jacket from the chair, pulling on her gloves, heading for the door.

"See ya," she calls, over her shoulder, leaving Barbara standing there, feeling like some dumb cartoon character, her hands out of control, as if they'd suddenly become too big for her.

It's 2:00 A.M. and Barbara wakes from a deep sleep, coming up with that funny feeling in her stomach, that falling sensation that's supposed to save you from hitting bottom in a dream of falling.

She's been dreaming of her dad tossing her up in the air, laughing. In the dream she had her adult face and a child's body. Her own, though it was dressed in a long, white christening gown with tiny, black, high-buttoned boots, like the pictures she'd seen of her mother as a child.

She comes up out of the dream into a memory of a circus. The Ringling Brothers and Barnum & Bailey Circus. Her parents had taken her sister and her when she'd been about six, but what she is remembering is going down to the fairgrounds in the morning to watch the tents going up. She remembers her dad waking them up when it was still dark outside and helping them bundle into sweaters and slacks even though it must have been late June. She can see the dim shape of their car in the driveway and feel the silent, rocking drive across town during which she drifted down against her sister's shoulder. Then her father shaking her gently again and swinging her up to his shoulders, the air so sharp and clear it was as if her lungs saw what was out there all of a sudden: men with huge coils of rope and the great, dark shapes of the elephants, four of them, kneeling to the long roll of canvas, pushing it forward.

She knows this is something that really happened – though she hasn't thought of it in years – but she can't tell now whether it was part of the dream or not. What happens next is that she puts her hand to her face and feels tears there, still wet, on her cheek.

Something is wrong. Something is wrong with Kate, but Barbara doesn't know what. Doesn't know what to ask, that is, or even if. And then what?

Right now she and Kate and Jason are sitting around the kitchen table, eating pizza. Or rather, Jason is wolfing it down, as usual, Barbara's putting away her share and Kate has been playing with the mushrooms on her piece for about fifteen minutes. Every time the phone rings (three times, already, twice for Barbara, once for Jason) Kate jumps up to answer it on the first ring. Now she's sitting on the edge of her chair, poised, like someone waiting for the starter gun in some weird race.

"You gonna eat that?" Jason looks hopefully from the empty pizza box to the piece on Kate's plate.

"No, you can have it. I'm not that hungry." Kate picks off the last mushroom and holds the rest of the piece out to him.

"Kate, you haven't eaten a thing." As soon as she says it, Barbara knows she should have kept her mouth shut. Kate's face closes against her. *Damn.*

"I'm fine, really. I'm just not hungry, okay. Besides, I'm thinking of going on a diet."

"Yeah, fatso," Jason talks with his mouthful, "you really need to diet; you're a mess."

"Jason! Kate, are you serious? You don't look overweight to me." Barbara can't help herself. Kate's never talked of dieting before.

Kate shrugs. "Just a few pounds, Mom. What difference does it make to you?"

"It's because of Danny, isn't it," Jason cuts in, enjoying his chance. "Last night, when he said you looked like Lois Campbell in that new skirt you had on." He stuffs the rest of the pizza in his mouth and leans back in his chair, puffing his belly out grotesquely, grinning at his sister.

"That was a joke, Jason, and you know it! Lois Campbell weighs about two hundred pounds."

"Yeah, well, you weren't laughin'." Jason pushes his chair back and heads over to the fridge. "I dunno, Katie." He opens a can of Coke with a loud pop. "I don't know what you see in that jerk, I . . . "

"Jason!" Kate and Barbara yell at him, together this time.

"Okay, okay." He holds up his hands good-naturedly, and heads upstairs to his room.

Kate turns back to the table. "You like Danny, don't you Mom?"

The question takes Barbara by surprise, it comes so easily. But Kate is playing with the flap of the pizza box, keeping her eyes down, concentrating. *Be careful.*

"I think he's nice, Kate." Barbara pauses, wanting that to be enough, at the same time as some other part of herself, some kind of invisible antennae, tests the air between them, delicately searching for an opening . . .

"And I know he really matters to you, Katie. A lot." She reaches, finally, into the space, this new space, that seems to have opened between them, overnight. *There. Now what?*

Kate's face holds its new, polished stillness for a moment. Then, it gives. Gives in, maybe. What Barbara already thinks of as the "old Kate" shadowing into her daughter's face, the way sometimes she sees some aspect of her own father there, or Norm, or herself. Something familiar and certain, no matter what.

"Oh, Mom, I really like Danny. It kinda scares me, you know. I mean, it's so, so *amazing*." She looks over at her mother again, almost smiling this time.

"Amazing?"

"Well, Danny Saunders." She stops, as if the name alone invokes everything she needs to say.

"Oh, I don't know, Kate. You've always had lots of boys around, lots of friends."

"Not really, Mom." Karen's voice is impatient now, an adult talking to a child. "That's what you like to think, but it's not true, you know."

If this were a just world, Barbara thinks to herself, as she watches Kate's face arrange itself to fit this new tone, there would be a script for moments like these. Not only what to say, but how to know what's being said somewhere outside of the words.

"Kate, I'm worried about you." It's all she can think of. But it works. Something makes Kate look at her, hard.

"What?"

What then?

Barbara can't put her finger on it. "Oh, I don't know," (mumbling, a child who's finally got her mother's attention) "all this . . . this dieting and all."

"Oh, Mother, for godssake – " but the phone rings then. Of course. And, of course, it's Danny. And, of course, Kate is gone again. "Just for an hour. He's got the backdrop finished and he wants me to take a look at it, right away."

"No, not Kate!" Barbara wakes herself up, calling out, from a nightmare. A field of high grass or a marsh. Her running through it, holding a child high over her head, the muscles in her back tearing with the effort, something snatching at her ankles, her body pitching dizzily forward as the child spins out of her arms, its face turning towards her, huge, coming into focus.

Kate.

She can see Kate coming downstairs last night, in her blue sweatshirt, her hair still a little damp at the tips from her shower. But that wasn't it. No, that wasn't what made it look, well, *off*, somehow, dull, like wet silk.

You mustn't go out with your hair still wet; you'll catch your death. Here, let me feel your forehead.

She looks at the bedside clock. Half past four.

Ten-thirty in Norway.

By the time she gets through to the plant in Sundelsora, to the right department, to the right secretary, it's almost five o'clock.

"No, I'm sorry Mrs. Huntington. Your husband's not here; he's gone out to Kristiansund till Friday. A meeting with some of our other people there. I can give you the number, but he did say if you called to tell you he'd call around midnight Friday. Our time, of course. Do you still want that number . . . "

"Yes, please."

The secretary in Kristiansund says he's running a test.

"Would you like me to page him?" she asks, but with that "give-me-a-break-lady" bite to her voice that Barbara can recognize – even through the accent and the static – as the one she employs when some kid wants her to haul a teacher out of class just to sign a green slip.

But honest, Mrs. Huntington, I gotta have it by next period or I lose a credit. Honest.

She feels like a kid herself.

Honest, I gotta talk to him. I've had a bad dream.

"No. It's not that important. Tell him I'll talk to him Friday, as arranged. Thank you."

"Fine then, Mrs. Huntington."

As the connection clicks down, she has a sudden image of Norm, surrounded by men in white lab coats, standing beside some huge press – sort of like those ironing machines at the cleaners, only larger – watching these sheets of metal spill out, thinner and thinner. He's got his back to her, the back of his head, dear, familiar – that place where his hair always sticks up so foolishly because he has a double crown close enough to touch. But he doesn't turn around.

She's shivering all of a sudden as if she's coming down with a cold. No point trying to sleep anymore. She grabs her dressing gown and drags herself into the bathroom for a long, hot shower. But it seems to take hours for the water to feel warm on her shoulders and she stands there, hugging herself like a little kid who's stayed in swimming too long. More than anything, she wants to go back to bed for the day. When she opens the bathroom door, she wants Norm to be standing there, surprising her as he sometimes does, flowers in one hand, a coffeepot in the other.

"What do you say we call in sick," he always says. "Let's play hooky, just you and me."

More than anything, she wants that.

Something is wrong. Something is very wrong for her daughter, Kate, and Barbara knows it. Knows it, but doesn't believe it.

No. Scratch that. She believes it all right. She just doesn't know what to do about it.

Like tonight. She's bundled on the couch with a hot-water bottle and a drink, watching TV, when Kate and Danny come in. They've brought a treat, Black Forest cake from the coffee shop and take-out cappuccino in

Styrofoam cups. Danny drapes his scarf over his arm for a napkin, bowing to Barbara as he serves her cake and coffee, turning it into an event, so compellingly good-natured it's hard not to like him. Kate turns the volume on the TV down, leaving the picture on so they can watch for the local news. They're supposed to be doing a promo piece on the play tonight.

The kids sit on the floor at either end of the coffee table, Barbara in the middle, like a tea party. On the screen people are earnestly holding up bottles of motor oil or fabric softener. Only these days it's not always who you expect doing what. Sometimes the women check the oil, the men pull the towels from the drier and hold them up to their noses.

The Black Forest is absolutely slathered in whipped cream.

And Danny really is charming.

So maybe she's making too much out of the way her daughter's face seems to be operated by remote control, fading out every once in a while, then coming up again when her eyes flick to Danny's. Maybe that's not what's going on at all.

Even when she feels it, right there in the room, when she sees how Kate's face – turned up to hers, laughing in the middle of a funny story – stops suddenly, her whole face, just stops at some movement from Danny's hand she doesn't even notice. Then he turns up the volume on the TV . . .

". . . the Northgrove production of *Pygmalion*," the announcer is saying.

The play, of course. They're so excited about it. But that still isn't enough for her to ignore it. What she sees in the way Kate lowers her head slightly like . . . like a small child being scolded, her face collapsing for a moment, as she turns, away from her mother, to the face on the TV.

Friday morning, Barbara is up at six o'clock and ready to go out the door by half past seven. She wants to set up a few things at the office before picking up her parents at the hospital, lay out the attendance forms so that even a goldfish could follow them. She figures this'll give Marnie a fighting chance.

She's just putting on her boots in the front hall when she hears Jason stumble into the bathroom. Silence from Kate's room. She was out late last night and she's been excused from classes, Barbara knows, from now until the play opens next Tuesday. Best let her sleep.

MEWS gives a sharp beep that seems loud enough to be real, outside, in *this* world, but Barbara shakes her head. Saturday. She's promised herself. There's no rehearsal, Kate will be home all day. And besides, tonight Norm will call. If she tries it out on him first . . . She imagines him going over it with her the way she imagines him going over things at work. Getting everything right, everything running, running smoothly again.

She gets to the hospital ten minutes early and, thank god, there's a parking place right near the door. As the door slides shut behind her, hospital heat closes in, hospital smell, white and antiseptic with its familiar, sweaty underwhiff of fear. Barbara loosens her coat and starts across the lobby to the row of elevators in the corridor. She's halfway there when one of them opens, spilling out the expected assortment of patients: a burly man on crutches, his ankle in a cast; a woman with a neck brace; a little girl, holding her mother's hand, her other arm hammocked in a fresh, white sling. Barbara's almost past the group before she sees the couple, there, at the back. Before she's caught by the woman's navy coat and queer, halting walk, the way she stops every step or so to twist herself around, surprised at the progress she is making.

Or rather, *they* are. Her husband's clamped to her right arm, his left leg dragging slightly as he walks. A big man whose clothes seem to flap around him, absurdly, as if he's just that moment shrunk inside them, like someone caught out doing something he never thought he'd have to, ashamed to be seen . . . by me, Barbara realizes, recognizing them slowly and with great difficulty, like someone in a dream, recognizing her parents. She stops just as her mother stops, her face startled into a smile.

Her father bumps up behind, staggers slightly, rights himself. "Oh, there you are, Barbara," he says teasingly. "Don't mind us." He gives her a wry smile, as if he, too, has just caught on to the fact that the people he trusts are no more certain than he is.

Or at least that's what Barbara thinks. That's why she laughs. And for a moment the three of them stand there, laughing at each other.

"The car's right outside, you two," Barbara says then, taking her dad's arm, still surprised to find it smaller, even, than she expected, lighter and thinner than she ever thought it could be.

He's scared, she thinks. And then: *As scared as I am.*

Terrified, at first, to have admitted that and, then, strangely reassured. To know that she has no other choice now (after she's driven her parents home, got them settled, gently refused their offer of coffee), no other choice but to drive back across town to her own place, kick off her boots and head up the stairs, two at a time, unbuttoning her coat as she goes. Open Kate's door and stride to the bed where her daughter is still huddled under the blankets like a small child. All she can do. To pull off the covers and find what she knew would be there, though not what to expect.

Not any of it. Not the size of the bruise that fills her daughter's cheek and pinches her left eye closed.

Not the way Kate turns to look up at her, her nose caked with blood.

Not how her own voice comes, finally, up from her chest, thinned by the work of pushing through her fear that it might not work at all.

"Did Danny do this to you?"

Her own need, really. To say it.

Kate is already crying. She holds her arms out, stiff and shaking, as if she's afraid of what she might get. As if asking for comfort feels like asking to be forgiven.

Leaving Barbara nothing more to do than this – climb into bed and curl her body around Kate's in the shape they both know by heart, settling easily into it. Both of them crying, as they will, off and on, for the next hour or so, until Barbara feels her daughter's shoulders loosen, a little, towards sleep.

That's when she reaches out to push Kate's hair gently back from her face. Holding her own face down to it for a moment, sniffing out sweat and sleep and perfume, and there, below that, the other scent she knew she'd find, what or how she couldn't tell you, not in words.

Though she knows it. As she knows her own smell. As she knows how to lie there, holding her child in her arms, letting her shoulders ease themselves into a position they can keep for hours if they need to, relaxing into it, trusting it to be enough.

Not for good, certainly, but at least for now.

AN EASY LIFE

Right now, Marion is giving her kitchen its once-a-year major cleaning, right down to that little crack where the gunk builds up between the counter and the metal edge of the sink. She's going at it with Comet and an old toothbrush, singing along to the Talking Heads on her Walkman, having a great time. She smoked a joint with her coffee before she started this morning. It helps. She's already done the fridge, the stove *and* the oven, wiped down the walls. Just the counters and drawers to go, really. Then the floor. Marion does a little dance over to the cupboard for the Lysol.

It's a beautiful day. The patio door is half open and the air that blows in is real spring air without that underscent of snow. Crocuses glow in creamy pools of purple and gold, all along the stone path to the garden. Soon, there'll be daffodils, tulips. And hyacinths, Marion's favourite, their sweet, heavy scent filling the kitchen, outrageous, it always seems to Marion, like the smell of sex.

Marion has thick auburn hair and the fine, almost translucent complexion that often goes with it. These days, she's got it cut short with longer wisps over her forehead and at the back of her neck. She has always been beautiful, not in any regular, classic way, certainly, but because she has the kind of bone structure that can give a face movement. At forty-two, her beauty seems deeper, more complex than it ever was, as if it's just beginning to discover all its possibilities. Everyone who knows Marion acknowledges how beautiful she is. The other thing they say is that she seems to have a very easy life.

She was born Marion Patterson, the youngest of three, the only daughter of a Home Economics teacher and a high school principal. Her health was always excellent, her teeth straight. She watched "Howdy Doody" and "Father Knows Best" and saw the first-time appearances on "The Ed Sullivan Show" of both Elvis Presley and The Beatles. In school she was one of those people who manage to get high marks without being a browner and at the same time is pretty, popular and good at sports.

All of this had its predictable effect when she entered university. After her first class, English 101, Marion walked directly to the centre of the campus where a long-haired boy with deep-set, deep-brown eyes was handing out leaflets. END CANADIAN COMPLICITY IN VIETNAM, they said. Below that was the time and place of a meeting. Marion took a leaflet. She also went to the meeting.

By Christmas she was spending most of her time in the coffee shop reading *Ramparts* and *I.F. Stone's Biweekly*, and talking to anyone who would listen about what she read. She wore short skirts, fishnet stockings and turtleneck sweaters in dark colours. Her hair was long then, straight down her back, almost to her waist, and her face was sharper than it is now, vibrant in an almost aggressive way that some men found intimidating.

One man who was not intimidated was Carl Walker, a second-year art student who spent his afternoons in the coffee shop smoking and sketching. Marion had one of the strongest profiles he'd ever seen. In April, Carl and Marion were arrested at a demonstration outside the U.S. Embassy in Toronto.

That summer they were married. Marion wore a long, red Indian cotton skirt, a tie-dyed T-shirt and a crown of daisies and black-eyed Susans. Carl wore blue jeans, a loose white shirt and a button that said, L.B.J. L.B.J. HOW MANY KIDS DID YOU KILL TODAY? Back at school, their tiny apartment was the favourite hangout of campus politicos. Carl made huge pots of chili, Marion rolled the joints and everyone argued with their mouths full. Over the stereo was a poster showing the profiles of Karl Marx, Mao Tse Tung and Ho Chi Minh. SOME PEOPLE TALK ABOUT THE WEATHER, it said above the profiles. And below, in larger letters, WE DON'T.

When Marion got pregnant, she and Carl decided to quit university and find a place in the country. They could grow their own food, Carl would continue painting, Marion would read.

"Who needs a degree?" Marion said.

"Just you wait," replied Marion's women friends, among whom feminism (or Women's Lib as it was then called) was making rapid advances. "Wait'll you have a colicky baby and it's thirty below outside. Carl'll go on painting the great male masterpiece and you'll be up to your elbows in shit."

Not so, however. Jason Dylan Walker was rapidly followed by Benjamin Joplin and Joshua Guthrie. All of Marion's labours were short, the boys were born undrugged, screaming red and perfectly formed. Carl was always there. He was – and still is – an enthusiastic parent, willing to do his share. He also kept on painting and managed to mount two highly acclaimed shows in six years. His paintings began to sell for very respectable prices.

Both Marion and Carl took pride in their organic vegetable garden and were keenly involved in a protest that stopped Ontario Hydro from building transmitter towers through a strip of choice farmland in their community. Marion raised chickens, Carl baked bread and they both spent hours taking the boys for walks in the woods around their farm. When Josh was five, Marion decided to go back to school. Carl's growing reputation got him an excellent faculty position in the art department of a small community collge, they moved into the city and Marion got her Masters in Psychology and Education. For the last five years, she has been a guidance counsellor at Centennial Secondary School. She is good at what she does. Not only do most of the kids like her, they sometimes listen to some of what she has to say. What's more, some of what she has to say is actually relevant to their lives as they see them.

Of course, Marion and Carl argue, who doesn't. And sometimes they both wonder what it would have been like if they'd waited a while, met other people, maybe travelled a little, if they hadn't been, well, so *young*. On the other hand, they also believe you have to go with what's happening at the time. Surprising as it may seem, this attitude still works for them.

Or so Marion says.

"Oh, Marion," her friends reply, only half-laughing. "Wake up. Look around. The sixties are over."

Marion knows what they're getting at, of course. For every Marion Walker, married at eighteen and having three kids bang, bang, bang, who ends up cleaning her spacious kitchen in her tasteful house on her tasteful street, a little stoned and more beautiful than she was twenty years ago, there are thousands of others with their teeth rotted and their bodies gone to flab on Kraft Dinner and Wonder Bread, up to their eyeballs in shit. Women whose husbands left them (as, in fact, Marion's own brother, Jeff, left his first wife, Sandra, with a three year old and a set of twins, with no degree because she'd worked to put him through med school and with support payments based on his last year as a resident rather than his present salary as a pediatrician), or, worse yet, women whose husbands are still around, taking it out on them, women who are beaten, whose kids end up in jail or ruined by drugs or . . .

Or take Tracey Harper, for example. She's just come home from her Saturday afternoon shift at Harvey's. The kitchen is scrupulously clean, as it always is, and on the table, in exactly the same spot as last Saturday and the Saturday before and every day after school for as long as she can remember, is a note in her mother's thick, wavery writing: *"Your supper's in the fridge. Just heat and eat. Love, Leslie."*

In the living room, the television is on full-blast, as always, "Wheel of Fortune" is half over and Leslie is sprawled on the couch, sound asleep, mouth open, snoring. On the table beside her, in a row, is a bottle of Maalox, a bottle of Coke, a bottle of rum, an empty glass and an empty package of Export "A"s. If Leslie were still awake, which would be unusual, she would light a cigarette, take two drags, put it in the ashtray, take two sips of rum and Coke, a sip of Maalox, two more drags of her cigarette and so on, never breaking her pattern until she ran out or passed out, whichever came first. It's by the same rigorous adherence to a system that she manages to keep her kitchen clean and food on the table for her daughter.

In so doing, she has done one helluva lot better – and she would be the first to tell you this – than her own mother. Like Tracey, Leslie came home to her mother passed out on the couch and the television blaring. Where Tracey stands in the doorway and watches men and women win glamorous merchandise and large sums of money on "Wheel of Fortune," Leslie would stand and watch women's wildest dreams come true, right there, on "Queen For a Day." What's changed (besides the television shows, of course) is that Tracey comes home to a clean kitchen and a meal, whereas Leslie came home to a shithole and nothing to eat. The other thing that's changed is that she, Leslie, has managed to keep her boyfriends out of Tracey's bed, which is more than her mother ever did for her.

What hasn't changed (besides the idea that winning something will improve your life): Tracey's eyes and her way of standing in the doorway, both of which are exactly like her mother's. Already she has the look and posture of someone whose parents abandoned her early. It doesn't matter to what – drugs, alcohol, violence, madness or death – she has that look. That particular sadness which starts in the eyes and goes bone-deep, displacing all traces of the child she was, leaving the shoulders stiff and thin, all their suppleness and softness gone for good. The softness that some of us are allowed to carry (that Marion Walker carries, for example) a good distance into our lives.

So Tracey is standing in the doorway of the living room, waiting for her supper to heat up, watching her mother sleep. Her mother is only seventeen years older than she is, which makes her thirty-four, but she looks about sixty. Her belly bloats out over the waistband of her jeans and the skin that shows, in the space between her jeans and her T-shirt, is grey and puckered. If statistics are anything to live by (and surely they're as reliable as game shows), Leslie will be dead in five to ten years. *How* is still being decided by her cells. Will it be her stomach, where the ulcer has already made it's presence known? Her heart or her lungs, whose complaints she hears but manages to ignore? Right now, her cells are deciding her future.

As indeed Tracey's cells are deciding hers. If she goes back to her boyfriend Kevin's tonight after the movies, as she usually does, she will get pregnant. Everything in her body (the delicate balance of hormones controlled by her pituitary gland, the ripened ovum swimming in her right fallopian tube) is ready. In one sense, her pregnancy has already been decided. Statistically, it's almost inevitable. If it actually occurs, then, given that course of events which are so usual as to seem almost natural, Tracey may replace Leslie in a few years, exactly as she is – passed out, bloated on the couch.

Lately, though, Tracey is beginning to think that maybe it isn't such a great idea after all, dropping out of school and living together, which is what she and Kevin are planning to do as soon as he gets on at Petro-Can.

What she is hearing, under the chatter of the TV and her mother's snoring and the sausages hissing in the pan behind her and her own confused thoughts, is the voice of her guidance counsellor at school, Mrs. Walker, who is one of the weirdest people Tracey has ever met. Sometimes they don't even *talk*, for fuck sake, they go to the mall and try on clothes. Seriously.

But what Mrs. Walker is saying now inside Tracey's head is: *Well, really, Tracey, your marks aren't that bad, you know. And you've got more experience of life than most kids your age. What you've gotta decide is how you're going to use that to your advantage. Any ideas?*

And then Tracey is amazed to hear her own voice, there, inside her head. As amazed as she was last Wednesday, when she heard herself say: *Well, I always thought I might like to be a physiotherapist.*

Physiotherapist. Yeah, right. She'd just read it on one of those stupid pamphlets they have outside the guidance office.

That's not a bad idea, Tracey, Mrs. Walker is saying now, *I think you'd be really good at that. In some ways working with people who've been injured might be a little like helping your mom. Now you'd have to go to university, so we're going to have to figure out some money schemes but I . . .*

And then she goes on, laying it all out like it's possible, and now Tracey sometimes thinks that maybe it just is. She walks over to the TV, turns it off, goes to the couch and picks up the empty glass and the cigarette pack, butts the last cigarette, which is stinking up the ashtray. She takes the glass, the full ashtray and the empty pack to the kitchen counter, comes back and eases her mother's body gently along the couch a little ways so that her neck isn't cramped over the arm like that. Then she gets her sausages and macaroni from the stove and heads for her room.

Already, she's thinking she might tell Kevin she doesn't want to go out tonight, though it's hard to imagine having the nerve to actually say that to him. Right now, it's just sort of there, like a buzzy place, inside her head. Right now, she's just going to eat her supper and study for her math exam. Then she'll see.

Marion fills the sink with hot water, adds detergent and a few drops of Javex and dumps in the contents of the left-hand middle drawer, the one where she keeps all the stuff she hardly ever uses. Tea strainers, pie servers, cookie cutters, two ice picks and a couple of those things you use to make little scoops of melon for fruit salads.

"Melon ballers," the boys call them.

Outside, she can see Ben and Josh sorting stuff for a garage sale tomorrow, hauling everything into the driveway and organizing it into piles. Hockey sticks and skates, a huge box of Lego, Jason's old ten-speed, a bunch of flippers and some diving masks, tennis racquets, a badminton set, ski poles. They lift and carry the awkward bundles with ease, competent and serious. Even Josh is almost passed the gangly stage, almost completely at home in the body he'll live in for the rest of his life.

A body that seems so much like a stranger's to Marion these days, even as she watches him, his every movement familiar. It's hard to believe she used to take it so for granted. All of it. The rooting motions their mouths made when she picked them up to nurse. The ease with which she oiled and powdered their bums, handling their penises as casually as she'd handle her own breasts, pushing back their foreskins to check for redness, helping them aim over the potty when she was training them. It doesn't seem possible.

Marion wipes out the drawer with a damp cloth, empties the sink, starts drying the stuff and putting it back, automatically, still watching the boys. Sometimes she doesn't know and it scares her. She can feel it, inside, what she doesn't know. It's like when she miscarried between Jason and Ben and how, even before the blood came, from the very beginning, she knew something was wrong, terribly wrong and there was nothing she could do about it even though it was there, right there, inside her own body. She can feel the cold sweat of it, the way she felt it then, all over her.

And no one else seems to notice, that's what really gets to her, they seem to see her as, well, *finished,* somehow. Carl and the boys. Or the kids she sees at work, other people's kids, as precious and impossible as her own. That she should be expected, should get *paid,* to sit in an office and tell other people's kids what to do with their lives seems crazy to her sometimes. Crazier that they listen.

Ben and Josh turn suddenly and see her in the window. They wave vigorously and Ben gets onto his old skateboard, mouthing something Marion can't hear with the Walkman on and the window between them. She shakes her head, but he keeps on, tilting the skateboard wildly, his arms waving a crazy semaphore, insisting on her attention. It reminds her of when they were little, all crowded around her, and she'd send them outside, just long enough for a coffee or to talk to Carl for a few minutes. How every two seconds they'd be at the door, wanting her to watch something or do something.

It used to drive her crazy sometimes. Still does. Even now as she waves, shaking her head again, vigorously this time, she can feel that familiar pulse of irritation at her temples, quick and absolute as the swell of love that comes with it.

Anger and tenderness. That she can feel so many conflicting things, that she can know so little about anything she feels and still manage to appear a competent adult. Sometimes it scares her. Knowing there's no end to feeling like this, ever.

The best Tracey Harper can do right now is to crouch behind the chest of drawers in her bedroom and listen as Kevin bangs and bangs and bangs on the door to the apartment. Before, it was the phone ringing and ringing and ringing. Her mother has slept through it all, which, even for her, is amazing.

"All right, bitch. I know you're in there." Kevin gives the door a kick.

Silence.

Then Tracey hears him stomp down the stairs, she hears the outer door bang shut. In a few minutes his car squeals off down the street. Tracey can see it perfectly, the dark blue, rusted-out '78 Firebird and Kevin inside, his knuckles white around the steering wheel, really fuckin' pissed off.

For a minute she thinks of getting up, going out, trying to find him. It would be a lot easier than this is. She wishes she'd never met that fucking bitch Walker. Now she's going to have to spend her time avoiding Kevin, who will be on her ass every goddamn minute. Phoning her at all hours, following her to and from school. All she'll be able to do is ignore him and keep on walking.

Even when he grabs her arm, hard, next Friday afternoon and pulls her towards him. Even when she has to kick him, she won't speak, she'll just get the fuck out of there and keep on going. It's all she can do.

And it isn't Kevin's fault, either. Though he's acting like a jerk right now, he's an okay guy. Next week he'll get on at Petro-Can, and had he and Tracey gone through with their plan, everything might have worked out fine for them, statistics be damned.

As it is, Tracey will spend the next three weeks sitting silent in Marion Walker's office, not even looking at her, arms clamped around her chest as if it takes her whole strength to hold its contents in.

She will look a lot the way she looks now, crouching against the wall of her bedroom, hugging her knees to her chest as if the effort of keeping them from jumping up, running into the hallway and never stopping till she finds Kevin, wherever he is, takes everything she's got.

Which it does.

Drawers and counters done, Marion goes to the cupboard for the pail and sponge mop, but before she starts the floor, she fills the coffeemaker and turns it on so that it will be ready when she is. She puts a new tape – *Patsy Cline's Greatest Hits* – into the Walkman and gets down on her knees to do the tough spots near the sink and under the edge of the stove. A whiff of Lysol stings her nose. Once the hard stuff's loosened, she does the rest with the mop, singing again, having a great time.

Sometimes what Marion thinks is simply that she's lucky to have such an easy life. "Karma" some of their friends used to call it, hanging out at the farm, smoking black hash, letting the boys run naked through the fields.

Other times she knows damn well it's because of Carl and their double income, her education, her parents' double income even, everything that's made her luck possible. Political, not spiritual, and she should damn well face up to what that means. Whatever that means.

Sometimes she just doesn't know, and it scares her.

Besides, who knows what will happen next, even in an easy life. In five minutes, for example, Jason will be driving in from the mall where he works part-time as a clerk at Music World, speeding, already late to pick up his girlfriend, Karen. While in an apartment nearby, someone else knocks back his last beer and climbs into his car to go get more before his friends show up. Two cars, both driven by teenage boys, hurtle towards each other, like sonar blips on a great map of possibilities, like cells gone haywire. Marion's own death ticks in her cells as it does in anybody's. Anything can happen, any time.

Still crouching behind her dresser, Tracey Harper has fallen asleep. She is dreaming. In the dream she is in a red Corvette convertible, moving very fast along a highway which is like a highway in a cartoon show, with flowers springing up on all sides, and birds and rainbows filling the sky. Mrs. Walker is driving and the two of them are laughing and eating triple-scoop French chocolate ice-cream cones from Baskin-Robbins. The dream is so vivid that Tracey can taste the cold chocolate on her tongue and feel the wind in her hair. She can hear herself laughing and laughing, and in the dream she reaches over and puts her hand, just there, for a moment, on Mrs. Walker's arm. In the dream, she has no idea where they are going.

Meanwhile, a few blocks away, Jason pulls up in front of Karen's place, gets out of the car and goes around to the back porch where she is waiting for him in brand-new, acid-washed jeans and a yellow sweatshirt, one of her mother's daffodils stuck behind her ear.

Meanwhile, Marion's kitchen gleams, the sun shines through the window, the crocuses pulse and shimmer as the afternoon wanes. Marion pushes the mop and pail into the corner and tiptoes around the edge of the floor to the coffeemaker, pours herself a cup and tiptoes back towards the patio door.

The breeze feels wonderful on her hot face. She wipes the sweat off her forehead with the back of her hand as she steps out, and that for some reason makes her think of the day she took Tracey Harper to the mall because she couldn't think of anything else to do and how they'd tried on clothes and makeup in The Bay. Tracey wanted to do Marion's face and she let her though she never wears makeup. Now, she can feel Tracey's fingertips again on her eyelids and her cheeks. They stick slightly, pulling at her skin, as if Tracey is pressing too hard, exasperated with something she sees there, something she can't erase or alter. And at the same time, they flutter and soothe, almost as a lover's would.

Anger and tenderness. From nowhere, Marion feels the tears start. On the Walkman Patsy Cline is singing one of those songs that someone sings when they've been ditched, trying to cram a lifetime of pain into every note.

And so Marion just stands there, on her patio, with a cup of coffee in her hand, crying like an idiot. Partly because of the song. Partly because it's finally spring and she's a little stoned. Because of her kids and her job. Because she's like that, Marion, soft and open, in her easy life.

But not only because.

TIP OF MY TONGUE

Dr. Carleton, my periodontist, likes you to call him Steve. The breezy informality of Steve goes with his hi-tech, open-concept office, with the exotic plants, the FM rock and the young, blonde dental hygenists wearing dusty pink or mint green lab coats over their designer jeans. They also wear surgical gloves these days, because of the AIDS scare, but there's nothing serious or medical about them, not in Steve's office. No. They're *flavoured* gloves, if you can believe it. Strawberry or cinnamon. Who invents these things?

Probably the same person who designs the posters they have tacked up on the ceiling, the ones you're supposed to chuckle over as they scrape away at your plaque. I'm under one called "Murphy's Law and Its Variations."

"If anything can go wrong, it will."

"Murphy's Law of Government: If anything can go wrong, it will do so in triplicate."

"Murphy's Law of Insurance Rates: What goes up, stays up."

My father had this joke he used to haul out whenever my sister Jill and I were going for a dental checkup. He'd open our mouths, peer in and say very, very seriously: "Well, ma'am, your teeth are fine, but your gums will have to come out." It was part of the ritual – like my mother taking us to Lawson's for a sundae afterwards – a way of cajoling us into participating willingly in our own pain.

Today, however, no one's going to take me for a sundae afterwards. And my gums *do* have to come out.

Well, not exactly.

They have to be slit and peeled back from the roots so that Steve can scrape away the bacteria that has deposited itself in little pockets under my gums and is now eating away at the roots of my teeth, which will fall out tomorrow unless I come up with the fifteen hundred bucks to pay for this, this *procedure*, as Steve calls it, which is obviously going to hurt like hell.

This is not exactly how Steve puts it, of course. He manages to make the whole thing sound stylish and carefree like blow-drying your hair. He even draws little diagrams as he sits beside me, or rather over me, since he has not returned my chair to its upright position and all I can see from here is his Adam's apple and his nose hairs. I can also taste my own blood, its saltiness mixed with the antiseptic, strawberry taste of his surgical gloves and the sweetish rot of the bacteria he's scraped away from my gum line just so I can see how bad it really is.

Steve wears a white dentist's jacket over *his* designer jeans, but he lightens it up with bright shirts and ties. Shades of fuchsia today, which look great with his carefully tousled blond hair and clear complexion. I'll bet he jogs. I'll bet he swims lengths at lunchtime, for godssake. I'll bet he eats bran for breakfast. I'll bet he flosses his fucking teeth every fucking night of his perfectly plaque-free life. That's the thing about good old Steve. He's got his priorities perfectly straight. Like his teeth. Look at him. Getting into periodontia just as it hit the big time. You hardly ever heard of it fifteen years ago, but now that they've pretty well wiped out tooth decay, they can get down to the gums.

Like cancer, right? You didn't get that as much a hundred years ago because you got TB instead. But no matter what you call it, it's still death and decay and you're still stuck with it.

Stancy Bradshaw, my next-door neighbour, says that my hostility towards dentists must come from some anger seeded deep in my childhood. She says that the mouth is a place of primal power and that those who touch the insides of our mouths touch our unconscious. A year ago, Stancy wouldn't have been caught dead saying something like "primal power." But then her husband left her and Stancy met this guy named Ernest – that really is his name – and Ernest took her to some "Harmony Weekend" somewhere and now Stancy can talk about stuff like aura balancing and soul readings *and* drink her coffee at the same time. It's amazing. She says if I just open myself and let her guide me, we can find this anger I have for dentists. The way she talks makes me see it as some sort of insect-like thing, curled up in a pocket of my lung or a curve of intestine, dark and resistant.

"You can talk to it," Stancy says, "you can touch it, play with it, forgive it. And when you're ready, you can let it go. It's so lovely when you do. Each night before I go to bed, I travel all through my body, every organ, every cell, speaking to all the angry things that entered me that day. And then I release them. I feel now that my body is filled with white light."

Stancy is blonde, fair-skinned and stringy. She used to wear wonderful reds and corals and bright blues, but then she got this message that these colours were blocking her energy. Now it's white for Stancy – and a pukey yellow which make her look like someone who's been on chemotherapy for about six months. *She* says she feels great. As a result of simply changing the colours she wears, she has experienced a deep, spiritual change as well. She says that – "spiritual change" – in the same way that she talks about reaching my anger, her voice steady and matter-of-fact, like someone talking about vitamins or the proper way to clean your teeth. A sort of hygiene of the unconscious.

Frankly, it makes me gag. It reminds me of my father's tapeworm story. He used to tell us about how people were cured of tapeworms by being starved for weeks and then having their mouths pried open and a saucer of milk held to their lips. The worm would crawl up their throats and stick its head out, someone would grab it, twist it off and the rest of the body would die inside. I don't know if my father really believed this or if it were just another one of his jokes, but it was horrible the way he told it, holding his cupped hands up to his mouth to demonstrate. My bowels clench, remembering. My teeth clench, listening to Stancy going on and on about cleansing your anger. As if it were a goddamn parasite, something you could purge yourself of, easily and for good.

The dentist I went to as a child was Dr. Allan. His waiting room was small and dark, furnished with green leather chairs and highly polished tables. The smells were of antiseptic, furniture wax and the crisp mixture of starch and talcum powder that surrounded Miss Hedron, Dr. Allan's assistant. In one corner of the room stood a glass case filled with stuffed birds. An owl perched at the top of the tree branch, which almost filled the case, and below him were sparrows, juncoes, robins and chicadees. In the empty space at the left, a cardinal flew, wings outstretched, towards the perch that remained forever in the future.

My sister and I perched on the edges of the big, thick chairs waiting for Miss Hedron to summon us.

"I have to pee," Jill would say, every time, clutching desperately at her crotch. "I'm so scared I have to pee again."

She said this in her usual, everyday voice, no matter who else was in the room. She never seemed embarrassed. Or maybe she was still young enough to say such things without being aware of the effect they caused. I prodded her in the ribs, but she ignored me.

"I have to pee. Bad."

"You don't think you can wait till later?" My mother acted as if all this were taking place in our living room at home.

"No. I have to pee right now."

And so my mother would take her out the door and down the hall to the washroom, leaving me to deal with the smiles of the other people in the waiting room. Conspiratorial, they seemed to me, those adult smiles, inviting me to share the joke. But I never got it. I picked up one of the weathered magazines and held it stiffly in front of my hot face.

National Geographic. Life. The Saturday Evening Post. I liked the covers on the latter best. Norman Rockwell. Especially the one where a freckled, red-haired boy watched anxiously while a fatherly vet taped his dog's ear. You could tell everything was going to be fine. Once, though, there was a cover with a stocky policeman hunched anxiously in a dentist's chair exactly like Dr. Allan's. He looked like a kid himself, that policeman, as he eyed the drill, poised to descend.

The drill that Dr. Allan used was nothing like the high-speed, high-whining things they have today. Ponderous, slow, it buzzed thickly inside my mouth. Clumsily, it seemed to me, like Dr. Allan's thick, dry fingers. Dr. Allan's fingers had a slightly pepperminty taste, and his breath, as he leaned over me, had the same sweet smell. Too sweet. Like medicine, it seemed to me, not candy.

Not something you could bite clean through to the centre of. There was a warning in that taste that made my throat close and my stomach heave as the drill moved closer to the spot, deep within my tooth, from which red-hot pain would sing along taut, fine wires to my fingertips and the backs of my knees. A soft spot, at the centre of my tooth which I thought I could feel, pulsing, like the soft spot on a newborn's head.

Our father insisted that we have our teeth filled without freezing, without even a whiff of laughing gas. He himself had had his appendix removed while he was wide awake, numbed only by a "spinal," as he called it, watching the whole thing – he insists he did – in the doctor's glasses. He believed that anaesthetics were bad for you, that they accumulated in the system like the chemicals used to preserve canned food.

"Formaldehyde. That's what they use to keep canned peas from rotting," he would tell us. "The same stuff they use to keep a dead body fresh. By the time the undertaker gets you, you're half-embalmed already."

In our house canned food was forbidden. So were white bread, chelsea buns, Cornflakes, Rice Krispies, chewing gum and candy. My father was a health-food faddist long before some guy in California invented crunchy granola. At breakfast we ate whole-wheat toast, rolled oats and millet and drank fresh-squeezed orange juice while our father lectured us about the dangers of bologna ("whipped blood and rodent hair," he called it), of dressing too warmly, of having too many blankets over us at night.

"Tough bodies build tough characters," he'd say. Which was why we weren't allowed anaesthetic at the dentist. We were building our characters.

"What kind of mothers will you be," he asked us once, "if you can't take a little pain?"

He didn't know about the sundaes afterwards, of course. It would have driven him crazy, the thought of all that white sugar coursing through our innocent veins.

"But what he doesn't know, can't hurt him." That's what our mother said. "And besides, it's only once in a while."

"Then why can't you just let us have freezing and not tell?"

"That's hardly the same, Lee. Surely you can see that."

I couldn't. What was more, I didn't want to. What I did want – from adults in general, my mother especially – was fuzzy and unpredictable, like the math problems Mr. Taylor wrote on the blackboard at school. No matter how carefully I copied them into my notebook, they made no sense when I got home. The need for clarity made me sullen and tenacious.

"But *why* isn't it the same?"

"It just isn't, Lee, that's all." My mother sighed and I knew, in the pit of my stomach, what was coming next. The clincher. "And besides, you know your father."

You know your father. What was that supposed to mean? I· thought of how my father left for work every morning. At precisely 8:15 A.M., he would get up from the table, rinse his hands under the tap in the kitchen sink and take his brown felt hat from its hook near the cellar door.

"Well, I'm off to the daily grind," he'd say. "How about a kiss for the working man?"

My mother would jump up and give him a peck on the cheek and then my father would wave to us – "Have a good day at school, girls" – open the cellar door, wave again and disappear downstairs to the basement.

To "The Shop" as he called it, a small room full of shelves and counters and hodgepodge, handmade tables. Every available surface was covered with radios, toasters, waffle irons, vacuum cleaners, lamps, blenders, juicers and irons. Wires spilled from cardboard boxes, screws and bolts filled cracked cups and on one counter, just to the right of the door, stood haphazard rows of shiny appliances, tagged and polished, ready to be picked up.

The people who came to our house, by the side door, said that my father could fix anything. "Your dad's fingers got x-ray vision," one man said to me once and I imagined tiny, invisible beams of light flowing from my father's hands to the spot where a radio spluttered and died or the gears of a razor locked.

I used to think it was magic, the way he could fix things. But lately I'd started to notice how his shoulders hunched, even when he wasn't prying and peering, his eyes squinting nervously as if he were trying to make the whole world fit inside a lamp base or a fan. It was the same look he gave to the mashed potatoes or the meat loaf: a queasy, suspicious look as if he suspected poison or worms or rot, as if he could smell some secret decay in every mouthful. The thought of him downstairs all day in his poky, smelly room embarrassed me, in the thick, hopeless way that Jill embarrassed me with her loud voice in Dr. Allan's office, the way my mother's calm embarrassed me, *letting her* go on like that. I kept my nose to my cereal bowl when he waved goodbye every morning, embarrassed for them all. Couldn't they see?

You know your father. I hated the way my mother played along with everything. She even kept the books, for "your father's business" she actually called it, going over his sloppy figures every week at her little desk in the corner of the living room where a television would have been, as far as I was concerned, if my father's business had been anything but a joke. Surely my mother *knew.* She kept the books for other businesses, after all. Shops downtown with glossy, colourful signs and clean windows in which their goods were respectably displayed. Sampson's Flowers. Blakeman's Leather Goods. Shops run by cheerful men who gave Jill and I charm bracelets or real diaries with keys at Christmas time, gloves or scarves for my mother, elegantly concealed in silver boxes with red, perfect bows. I loved the cool, sleek touch of those wrappings. It reminded me of the marble counter at Lawson's and, somehow, of the taste of the sundaes, themselves. The slow, secret luxury of chocolate sauce and ice cream, the sweet-tart sting of the cherry I always saved for last. My mother loved ice-cream sundaes; she made a great fuss over the scarves and gloves. How could she go along with my father then, with his crotchety jokes and his greasy, lumpy, old brown hat? It made me queasy, like the chocolate bars I smuggled into my room and wolfed down before I fell asleep at night. It made me sick, the thought of it, the thought of married life.

Pain in the mouth radiates, the way a canker always feels bigger and hotter and sorer when you touch it with your tongue. All those nerve endings, pulsing. Right now, the whole right half of my head is on fire, I couldn't open my mouth to say "shit" if my throat were full of it.

Good old Steve. He's probably in some fancy restaurant right now, eating lunch on the five hundred he made this morning, cleaning out the bacteria from the upper side of my mouth. "The upper right *quadrant*," Steve calls it, making torture sound scientific. I wonder if he thinks of all that slimy, smelly bacteria as he scarfs down on his sirloin. I wonder why anyone would go into periodontia in the first place.

I'm lying on the bed, waiting for the painkillers to kick in. Stancy dropped by earlier to see how I was. She held the bottle of pills Steve had prescribed for me at arm's length with this prissy, horrified look on her face, like she'd just discovered a bottle of arsenic on my kitchen table.

"This stuff is really bad for you, Lee," she exclaimed. "Are you sure this guy knows what he's doing?"

"Stancy, for chrissake, he's a goddamn *specialist*. It's his *job*. What am I supposed to do? It hurts like hell." Already, my mouth was burning and the freezing wasn't even out yet.

"Yes, but Lee, this just dulls the experience for you. It puts you out of touch with what's happening."

"That's fine with me, Stance. That's how I like to be when someone's scraped half my face off with a razor blade. Out of touch. The further out the better." I opened the bottle and popped two of the painkillers into my mouth before heading over to the sink for a glass of water.

"Lee! The label says *one*." Stancy was right behind me, close, as if she expected me to collapse on the spot. This is a woman who used to smoke two packs a day before she met Ernest. Three for the month after her husband left.

"Look, Stancy, I know this isn't what you'd do, but I'm in a lot of pain – and I've got papers to mark. I've got to be back at school tomorrow, you know." I used the tone I've perfected for my teenage children, a reasonable, hopeful tone that reminds me, at least, that whatever they are saying is just part of a phase, just something I have to get through. Like a trip to the dentist.

"But you could use your pain, Lee. You know, as a guide?"

"A guide? What to? Insanity? Jesus, Stance, lighten up, okay, just for today."

"But there's so much power there, so much . . . "

"Stancy. I mean it. Go!"

Stancy shrugged and grinned, letting a little of my old friend show through, making me hopeful for the future. We've been through a lot together, after all. She gave me a little hug and let herself out. I took another pill for good measure, raising my water glass to Stancy's retreating back as I did so. Then I headed for bed.

Finally, finally, the pills begin to work. The room is pulsing with light now, the plants in the window glow, suspended in midair. I'm feeling pretty good. The pain is still there, but distant, like an echo, like a memory of pain.

Primal power, my ass. Jesus, Stancy, do you think I don't remember, is that it? Do you think I don't *know*? I remember all of it. I just don't see the point, is all.

I was probably eleven or twelve the first time. I thought it was just a mistake, that he wasn't used to it or something. It was Miss Hedron's job, after all. But she was on the phone in her little cubbyhole off the waiting room, and when Dr. Allan undid my bib, his fingers brushed my chest. Ever so lightly.

Chest. *Breasts.* He brushed them with his hands, though you could hardly see them under my blouse. His touching them made them seem bigger, somehow. Clumsy, awkward and faintly ridiculous.

"There you go, kid," he said. "That wasn't so bad, now was it?" He always said that, like he expected you to agree with him. He made it seem like a joke we were sharing, but now I couldn't tell what it was I was supposed to get, if he was talking about the filling, which hadn't been that bad, or about touching my breasts with his thick, pepperminty hands. I shook my head and opened the door to the waiting room.

Jill and my mother already had their coats on.

"How was it?" my mother asked.

I could feel Dr. Allan in the doorway behind me, the damp, sweetish smell of his breath at the back of my neck.

"Okay, I guess," I mumbled.

"Fine, as usual, Mrs. Stewart," Dr. Allan said. "Just a tiny, tiny cavity this time. We're doing much better on the brushing, I can see that."

Miss Hedron came to the door just then and the three of them stood there, grinning like idiots as if I'd just answered the sixty-four-thousand-dollar question or something. I grabbed my coat and headed for the stairs. I wanted to get out of there, I wanted to think, I wanted it to be a mistake.

But it wasn't. No. It was a beginning. Pinches, brushes, light, moist touches. Breasts, buttocks, the dark, scary space between my legs, no matter how tightly I clamped them. Always quick, always without warning, no matter how hard I watched for it.

I never thought of it as sex. This had nothing to do with what I heard in the school yard or the stuff my friends and I gleaned uneasily from books and magazines. I would sit in that chair waiting for him to touch my breast, put his hand between my legs, but it was as if this had nothing to do with breasts or crotches. My breasts. My crotch. Dr. Allan's hand had nothing to do with those places. Always, he touched something darker, something more, more intimate, I want to say. The sharp bite of the drill hitting an exposed nerve.

"Dr. Allan's been feeling me up, every visit, for the last three years." I imagined saying this, out loud, in Lawson's, just after my mother had ordered the sundaes. "Feeling me up" was the perfect phrase. I imagined saying it in the clear, unembarrassed voice with which my sister Jill used to announce her need to pee. The voice of someone who doesn't give a sweet shit whose listening, someone who knows her rights.

But I never did. Who knows why? The responsibility, maybe. The embarrassment. My mother's calm. My mother. I tried to imagine the questions she would ask, specific, focused, physical. *Where did he touch you? With his hands?* And others, worse, names for things that I knew my mother would have no trouble pronouncing. Words she'd expect me to share, as if we were in this together. I wasn't up to it, to the questions, those bright needles of alarm piercing my skin.

Pain in the mouth radiates. Blunted, muffled by drugs, it drones on, a dark red disturbance, like a cloud, just at the edge of my sight. I drift in and out of sleep.

Below me, the household carries on. I hear the kids come home. A pizza is delivered, rock music pounds (softly, yes, but pounding still) from the stereo, the phone rings, again and again. It's always for Allison. Her voice reaches me intermittently, certain words making it through the general din. "Geek." "Dick-head." Even at this distance her tone is casual, almost lazy, as if she rolls the words on her tongue, tasting, deliberating. Deliberate. Just like my sister Jill.

"The old fart," Jill says, as we climb the stairs to Dr. Allan's office. "The stupid old fart." She has taken to talking like this lately when we are alone. Boldly and carelessly. She is not trying to shock anyone. This is just how she has decided to talk.

"The stupid old poky fart." She is talking about our father, who has just stopped the old Chev, cautiously, jerkily, at the corner to let us out before inching his way on down the street to the A&P. Our mother's bookkeeping business is much bigger now and, lately, it is our father who drives us to and from dancing lessons and dental appointments.

Not that we want him to. I am fourteen, Jill is twelve.
Even she can see. We roll our eyes at each other when
our father is driving, hunched over the wheel, talking
nervously to himself, twitching his head from side to
side like a rabbit. We'd rather take the bus, but he insists.
"You never know what can happen," he says.

No sundaes afterwards. That's what will happen. It is
summer, hot, our cotton dresses cling to our bums and
the back of our legs. We reach the top of the stairs. The
door to Dr. Allan's waiting room is open, as it always is.

"The flaming asshole." Jill says. Several heads jerk
towards the door.

It is even hotter in the waiting room than it was
outside. My dress sticks to the leather chair as soon as I
sit down. Just like the car seats. Already I can feel the
stuffy air of our old Chev as we drive home, all the
windows up because our father insists that the air
downtown is bad for our lungs. Already I can feel – in
the pit of my stomach – the tentative stop-start jerks as
the car moves forward. My father's quick breath.
The horns of the other cars, blaring as they swerve to
pass us.

Jill flings herself into the nearest chair. "The stupid old
fart." She doesn't even notice how the lady beside her
raises her eyebrows and purses her lips. She just sits
there, erect, glaring, legs apart, kicking at the magazine
table. It's her knees I notice, bony and abrupt. And it's
like I'm seeing her for the first time, how crazy and brave
she is, how she doesn't – really doesn't – care. And what
I want is for her to be like that always.

"Dr. Allan keeps feeling me up." I try the words out,
for the millionth time, in my head. Try to imagine myself
in the back seat of the car, releasing them into that air,

towards my father's hunched shoulders, the stiff cords of his neck, the way he strains forward as if the traffic lights won't change unless he watches them every second, with all his might. With all my might, I try to imagine it, but I cannot. And I realize then, and as if for the first time, the danger I am in. The extent of it, for both of us. For Jill and me.

Miss Hedron calls me in then, gets me settled in the chair, clips on my bib and lays out the instruments on the tray beside me.

"Dr. Allan will be with you right away," she says, the way she always does and then the phone rings and she is gone, and that is the moment when I reach up and grab one of the pics and hold it close to my side, under the folds of my skirt. I don't have a plan. Already the cool steel is slippery with sweat.

"Well, well, well, and how are we today?" Suddenly Dr. Allan is there, above me. "Ready for a ride?" He tips back my chair and adjusts the light.

I open my mouth.

Dr. Allan hums under his breath, as he always does, clicking his little mirror against each tooth in time.

"Well," he says, finally, "aren't we a lucky young lady. No cavities this time."

I close my mouth and lean forward so quickly that I almost knock the mirror out of his hand.

"Ah," he grins down at me, "big hurry today. I bet there's a boyfriend waiting downstairs, am I right?" He winks at me, as if this is a secret we share, this imaginary boyfriend. And then, suddenly, his hand slips between my legs. Even though I am tensed for it, it is still a surprise, cold and improbable against my thighs, which are suddenly huge and sweaty. His thick fingers bump against the bulge where my crotch pushes against my underpants, pulling at the damp cotton, catching at the tiny hairs, sending hot, stinging slivers into my gut.

And then it is like a dream and I am moving my fist up high and bringing it down hard and it hits. I feel the pic go through his shirtsleeve, crunch against his skin. There is a slight gasp and the hand is withdrawn.

"You little bitch." No adult has ever spoken to me in this tone of voice before, ever. But I recognize it. Once, in Lawson's, the man in the next booth used it on the woman with him. "You whore." I remember the jerk of my mother's head, the sharp ripples of warning that reached me, even before her look did. *Had I heard that?*

"You little bitch," Dr. Allan says again. "What in hell do you think you're trying to pull?"

"You know." It is all I can say. I have that swollen feeling in my face, like when I'm being scolded by a teacher.

"What do I know, exactly." Dr. Allan shoves his face at mine. I watch his eyes, but I don't know what to look for. Suddenly he reaches out and grabs my shoulder, hard. I can see the white rim of his cuff and, further up, a tiny ooze of blood on his sleeve. "Don't get any smart ideas," he says. His voice is raspy, rough with some emotion I cannot even imagine. "Just remember. No one's going to believe you."

He lets go of me then and turns to the sink to wash his hands. "Who were you going to tell anyway, sweetheart? Your father? That gutless crackpot?"

It's the scorn in his voice that reaches me now, not the words, though I hear them, but with some other part of my mind. It's his scorn that burns through, unexpected, like his touches, leaving me open and exposed. As if he has found his way in to something I thought was absolutely private, something no one else could see. It is as if he has been in our kitchen in the mornings and seen my father in his greasy brown hat as he waves us goodbye every morning. And when he turns back towards me, drying his hands on a soft, white towel, it is as if nothing unusual has happened, as if I am the one who must account for my clumsiness as I push myself out of the chair and stumble towards the waiting room.

When I open the door, Jill stands up, gives the table a final kick and shoulders her way past me.

But Miss Hedron is there, just behind me. "I'm sorry, Jill," she says. "And you, too, Mrs. Adamson," nodding at the lady in the other chair. "I'm sorry, but Dr. Allan is unwell. I'll have to reschedule you for next week." She closes the door to the office, walks across the waiting room to the outer door and stands there, waiting till we leave. Then she closes the door behind us.

"Well, isn't that pissy," Jill says as we start down the stairs. "And I could have gone to the beach with Lydia this aft." She pushes the heavy door open into the heat, which is thicker than ever. "What made him sick, anyway, the old poop. The sight of your ugly face, I'll bet."

She grins over at me and I want to tell her everything, explain what happened. What I think happened, anyway, my own uncertain order of events. But my mouth feels thick and unwieldy. The heat presses in on us as we lean against the side of the building, watching the street.

"Jesus, that's him," Jill says suddenly with a snort of laughter.

Across the street a skinny, fair-skinned man in a blue, short-sleeved shirt, waves his arms like wobbly sticks. He looks like he's been standing there for hours, waving desperately. At us. A few people turn to stare.

Jill and I roll our eyes at each other, link arms, and start across the street. We walk slowly, though, and not directly towards him, so that we manage to arrive at the car as if by accident. Or as if he just happened to be in our way. Our father, grabbing for our attention, like a tourist asking directions.

Morning. Sunlight wakes me, hitting my eyes from an angle I don't usually see, not on a workday. I grab for the alarm clock. Someone has stuck a note over the face.

"Don't worry, Mom," it says in my son's handwriting. "We've called in for you. Have a great day. Everything's under control."

Right. I lift the paper. 10:45 A.M. At this very moment, my Grade Nine-B's are driving some supply teacher up the wall.

Downstairs, the kitchen is clean, surprisingly, almost suspiciously clean. There's a full pot of coffee in the coffeemaker and beside it, a bowl of peonies, red ones, from the garden. Already, their outrageous scent has taken over the house.

I root around in the fridge, dig out the rest of last night's pizza and a couple of not-too-stale chelsea buns, stick everything in the microwave. By the time I've poured the coffee, breakfast is ready.

If only my father could see me now. But he's miles away, of course, and already at work, while my mother sits down with the one-half cup of coffee she allows herself each day.

"Rotgut," my father says. "And addictive, just like heroin." He's right, of course – and now he has a whole generation of Yuppies to support him.

I raise my cup in his general direction. And pour myself another. It's great to sit here like this, during the day, in an empty house. I haven't had the chance in years. The silence seems to expand, moving up and away from me through all the rooms.

And my mouth feels great. It's as if I've slipped out of the pain, as I would a T-shirt or a pair of underpants. I can almost see it, curled up under the bed with the dust balls.

I never told. Even later, at college, when it would have been one of those outrageous, hilarious stories we told each other over beer and pizza in the dorm. By then, I didn't even think of it anymore. It just didn't matter.

How do you know? That's what Stancy Bradshaw would say, of course. And she'd be right. After I stabbed him Dr. Allan never touched me again. I don't think he ever touched Jill. But how do I know? Perhaps what I don't remember is worse, even, than what I do. Perhaps my silence is like taking aspirin to shut off pain. Pain from an unknown source, pain that may be the sign of cancer. Or something else, something they can cure.

Stancy Bradshaw would even go so far as to say that what has happened to my mouth – this rot that eats away at the roots of my teeth – is really my own silence, eating away at me. She believes this, simply and wholly, the way she believes that the clear white light that fills her body every night flushes away all her anger. In her world, I shouldn't have to go to Dr. Carleton at all, my gums would heal themselves, if I would only speak up.

But why? Espcially now. Dr. Allan died two years ago and it was the kind of death Stancy could have scripted. My mother sent me the clipping from the paper. DENTIST'S DEATH RULED ACCIDENTAL was the headline. The article said he'd been found dead on his front walk, early in the morning. It was the middle of winter and he'd been there all night. Exposure, the paper said. Seems the old guy passed out walking to the house from the driveway. The next part was confusing, but you could get the general drift. Booze and nitrous oxide. Laughing gas. Good old Dr. Allan. "Easy work for the undertaker" – my mother had scrawled under the smeary photograph – "Ha. Ha."

In her note, she was a little more serious about it, as if she regretted what she'd written on the clipping. "Your father's very upset," she wrote. "And of course I am, too. The man had been carrying on like that for years, even at work. I can't help thinking of you girls and those drills and no freezing."

But you know your father.

I could hear her saying that to herself, as she wrote. Just as I said it as I read, finishing up for her. And for the first time it hit me how much it sounded like the punch line to a joke you don't have to tell anymore. A family joke, like the bit about the undertaker.

Before I know it, I'm digging around in the sideboard drawer where I keep her letters and I'm glad when I find that one. It seems important, suddenly, to look at it again, as if I've missed something, before. Something vitally important.

I can't help thinking of you girls and that drill and no freezing. Yes, it's there, she really did write it. What is she thinking of? I can feel it, in the pit of my stomach, how much I want it to mean, that sentence. How long I will sit here, puzzling over it. Family jokes. Family codes. All that stuff that keeps me stuck to them, to my father and my mother, to Jill. How I can't get rid of being me.

And how afraid I am of even this small offering, if that is really what it is. Acknowledgement, maybe, even apology. The most my mother will allow herself. Like her one-half cup of coffee every morning, after my father's gone down to The Shop.

PEOPLE YOU'D TRUST YOUR LIFE TO

". . . Every fuckin' night at eleven, no matter what. What's he think he's trying to pull?" Gail plunks the liquor store bag on the counter and begins emptying it, clinking the bottles so hard as she lines them up that Myrna is sure she's going to break one.

"But can't you just leave the room?" she tries gently. "It's only a TV show."

Gail strides over to the cupboard, yanks open the door, gets out two glasses. "What good would that do. I'd still know he was in there."

"But I do think you have to find some way of ignoring it, Gail, really. You can't let it get to you like this."

"But it *does* get to me!" Gail snaps a couple of ice cubes into each glass. "That's what I'm tryin' to tell you, goddammit!" She grabs the first bottle and gives the cap a good twist.

Myrna says nothing. She's not sure what to say. Up until now they've been treating this thing as a bad joke, she and Gail, this thing with Gail's son, Stephen. The kid insists on watching "Leave It to Beaver" reruns, religiously, on late-night television. Really. That's all.

"Oh, I don't know," Gail says, suddenly, wearily, as if she's been pestered into answering. "Maybe it's me. Maybe he's trying to tell me something and I'm too stupid to get it."

Myrna watches Gail's hands as they mix the drinks. How small they are, fine-boned and efficient, like every movement they make, so neat and predictable that Myrna almost believes she knows what they will do next. Even the scar on the back of Gail's right hand is part of what she is to Myrna now, an emblem of what has brought them together, a landmark in familiar country.

"So what do you think he's trying to tell you?"

"Oh, you know, all the usual stuff, the stuff you always worry about when you're like this. That I haven't done enough. I haven't given him a normal family." She hands Myrna a drink and sits down at the table with her own. "I don't know. I've told him everything I can, why we left, all that. I've even said if he wants to try and find Barry, I'll help him. But I . . . "

Her voice has something else in it now, something dark, and fragile underneath the anger. What, Myrna doesn't know yet. She reaches out and takes Gail's hand, feels the familiar roughness of the raised flesh, where the scar is, underneath her fingertips.

"Then you've done enough, Gail. Stephen will be okay, really."

Gail pulls her hand away and lights a cigarette. "Jesus, I'm getting all carried away and we're not even drunk yet." She raises her glass in a toast. "Here's to the Cleavers," she says with a little laugh.

Myrna raises her glass, too. "And Eddy Haskell," she shouts. "My favourite."

"Yeah," says Gail. Then she adds, almost as an after-thought, "Did you ever notice Ward wears a tie to dinner every night? Can you believe that, a tie to everyday dinner? Jesus" – she shrugs, more like her old self – "what's got into that kid?"

"Hi there! Am I late?"

Nina arrives just as Gail and Myrna are starting to think about seconds. Comes right in, leaving the doors open, carrying an enormous platter of her lemon-garlic chicken, which she puts in the oven, turning it on to low before going back out to the hall to get rid of her coat and boots. "Don't worry about the mess. I'll wipe it up in a minute."

Back in the kitchen now, on her knees with a paper towel, cleaning up her snowy, salty footprints. "Selena called, just as I was leaving. She'll be here by seven."

"What's she bringing?" Gail steps around Nina for the ice.

"Blueberry cheesecake with whip cream." Nina gets to her feet, puts the paper towel in the garbage and comes over to the table. "She tried it out on me last week. It's depressingly good. I know we'll eat it all. And she's dyed her hair blue," she adds, as if this is logically connected to Selena's prowess as a gourmet cook.

"Are you serious? Completely?"

"Well, not really. Sort of just the tips. But it has this blue shimmer, you know. It looks great."

"Only Selena." Myrna laughs.

"Exactly." Nina's own hair is dark and long and thick with curls. Tonight she's got it pinned up with one of those Day-Glo green plastic clips her daughter Kelly wears. She's wearing a green shirt of Paul's over some old, grey jogging pants that could be anybody's. And trailing around her neck, Isadora Duncan style, a wonderfully expensive, pink silk scarf.

It's the scarf that gets Myrna. The perfect Nina touch. She leans over to kiss her cheek as she sits down. Gail brings another round of Brandy Alexanders and a dry martini for Nina, who fishes out the olive first, pops it in her mouth and licks the gin off her fingers.

"There's something I need to tell you . . . " she begins, as Nina always does, not wasting any time. Myrna and Gail lean instinctively towards her, and Myrna catches the bright blur of their movement in the darkened window beside them. For a minute, they look like kids. Teenage girls at a slumber party, someone's folks out of town for the weekend.

But before Nina gets a chance to say anything, Selena arrives, wearing a blue leather knee-length tunic over what appears to be a set of men's long underwear, dyed blue. Blue stones shine from her ears and fingers, silver bangles tinkle on both wrists.

And her hair. Blue at the tips, almost completely white otherwise, great puffs and waves of it, haloing her face, covering her shoulders. She shimmers and shines, floats about three inches above the floor. For her, Gail has a special concoction. Selena's Blue Heaven, it's called. Ingredients: top secret. Colour: blue.

Selena Bluestone. Nina Sorenson. Gail Parker. Myrna Summers. Lifetime members of G5 (Good Girls Gobble and Gossip Group), which has met on the third Thursday of every month for ages now, no matter what. Once a month, one of them clears her house of mate and children, buys candles and flowers, and the four of them carry on, all night sometimes.

Carry on. As in, certainly: "to behave (reprehensibly), to talk volubly, to rail at."

And, less obviously: "to keep up, to advance, to move on."

". . . So I'm thinking maybe I should make him see somebody, you know, somebody who knows about this stuff," Gail says, as she helps herself to more of Nina's chicken. On to Stephen again. "He's gotta face up to what's going on here."

"What *is* going on, exactly, do you think?" Selena, of course, picking out all the mushrooms from the salad bowl, methodically, never letting anything get away.

"That's just it. I don't know. But I don't think it's healthy, that's all."

"What's not healthy about it?"

"Ah, c'mon, Selena, don't play dumb. It's been fifteen years since I left Barry. Stephen's eighteen, for chrissake."

"What's that got to do with anything?" Selena's voice keeps its irritating, calm persistence.

"Maybe it's that he *wants* it to be like that," Nina puts in, gently. "You know, like trying to fix up a memory. Don't you ever do that?" She looks around at them, grinning shyly, "I mean, change stuff, so it feels better."

Gail pushes herself away from the table and lights a cigarette. "Yeah, Nina. It's called denial. Psychiatric hospitals are full of people like that. So are the jails."

"Gail, really." Selena gets up, goes to the counter and brings back her cheesecake, laughing. "Listen to yourself. How do you know Stephen's not watching "Leave It to Beaver" to help himself *face* something."

"Are you serious?"

Selena shrugs. "You never know, do you? Now c'mon, forget Stephen. Pig out on the cheesecake."

But Gail won't give up this time. She folds her arms tightly across her chest, holding in, holding on. "I know it's crazy, but I can't help it. Watching him sit there, watching that crap." Her voice has its rough edge now, the edge the others recognize as the closest she will ever get to crying. So that they all fall silent, for a beat, on cue.

"What is it you're afraid of, Gail?" Selena asks softly. The only one who isn't afraid to ask, Myrna thinks, watching the way the light glints around her as she leans forward, puts her hands on Gail's arms, just above the elbows. Holds them there, waiting.

Myrna has known Selena through three incarnations, ever since she was Susie Patterson back in Grade Eight at Elmgrove Public. Three and a half, if you count the switch from Susie to Suzi in Grade Ten. At the end of Grade Thirteen, Suzi Patterson became Suzi Sims when she married Greg and started having her four boys while Myrna went to teachers college. They still saw each other frequently, and, when Myrna and Ron finally bought their first house, one of the considerations was the fact that Suzi and Greg's place was a few blocks away.

That summer, Myrna and Suzi spent almost every evening and all day Saturday at the park. Myrna's oldest, Clarke, and Suzi's youngest, Roger, were on the same baseball team. They were barely two months apart, but Roger looked about twice Clarke's size to Myrna, a solid, well-co-ordinated kid who never missed the ball and usually hit a home run.

Floundering in the depths of the outfield, Clarke seemed impossibly small. Small and daydreamy, staring at the sky or the grass while the ball sailed over his head or dropped through his too-late, half-hearted attempt at a catch. Once or twice the ball glanced off his shoulder, stunning him sideways; another time it hit his stomach, stopping the game momentarily, as he slid to the ground, silent and white.

Every game got worse instead of better as far as Myrna was concerned. She clung to the edge of the bench, biting her lips, trying hard not to cry out every time the ball came his way.

"Relax," said Suzi, pulling a beer from the small cooler she always brought with her. "None of these kids pitch hard enough to kill him. Besides, if he knows you're nervous, he's gonna be nervous, too."

"You're saying *I* make him a bad baseball player?" Myrna hated the way Suzi handed out these little bits of instant wisdom on raising kids. Her boys were regulars at

Emergency. Someone always had a cast on something or stitches somewhere. Myrna saw them as veterans of an endless and increasingly alarming conflict between the human body and various pieces of sports equipment. It was getting so she hated to ask what had happened. Suzi didn't seem to care anymore.

"I'm not saying that, exactly," she took a long swig from her beer before she answered, "but you might as well face the fact that the kid's gonna get hurt sometime and there's nothing you can do about it. You can't protect him from LIFE."

LIFE. In capital letters. That's how it sounded to Myrna anyway. Really.

But when Clarke did break his arm, it was Suzi who was there. Calm and cheerful – while Myrna felt the park spinning and sliding away from her, the way the arm dangled grotesquely from his tiny shoulder – showing him how to hold it tight to his body, getting them all into the car, finding Myrna's OHIP number when they got to the hospital.

And it was Suzi she turned to, later, when she found out she was pregnant with Brian. And didn't want to be, that was for sure. The kids were both in school, she was back teaching, she felt somehow that her life was her own again. She was five months gone before she realized what was happening. *Admitted* what was happening. To her.

"You could still have an abortion, you know," Suzi said quietly, when she told her. " Go to Syracuse. They'll do them up to six months at the clinic there."

"Suzi! It's moving! You know what it's like, how it's different after you've had a baby. I couldn't."

"You could if you wanted to."

Why was she always so goddamn sure of herself? "I couldn't. It's not like I have a choice."

"You always have a choice, Myrna. You just may not want to make it."

Judgemental as hell, really. But she was there. Always. And when Myrna called her late one night, drunk and hysterical at eight months, saying, "I want it to be dead. Fuck it. I want the goddamn thing to be dead," she didn't say, "Well you could have . . . " or "I told you so."

"I'll just put my clothes on," she said. "I'll be there in ten minutes." And she was.

From where she's sitting Myrna can see the driveway of the house next door and she looks out just as the tow truck pulls in. Again. Every night for a week now, she's noticed. The guy who drives it is about twenty-two, tall and dark with a firm, slim bum. The house belongs to the Andersons, but they're on sabbatical this year and they've rented it to a couple of women. Travel agents, Myrna surmises. Esprit sweaters and high heels. They come and go a lot with suitcases.

What Myrna figures is that one of them went off the road during that storm two weeks ago, on the way back from the airport. She imagines the darkness and the cold, the flying snow. The travel agent is wearing a light jacket and thin shoes, having just come back from a Fam-trip to Jamaica. And then this guy shows up in his tow truck. He hauls her car out and follows her home, just to make sure she's okay. The travel agent asks him in, she has a bottle of Jamaican rum in her suitcase and it's such a cold night. One thing leads to another and there you are.

Myrna raises her glass to the young man as he gets out of the truck and starts up the walk. To rescue. To romance.

Gail makes the best Brandy Alexanders Myrna has ever tasted. It was also the first drink Gail ever made for her after she'd started her bartending course.

"What'll it be?" she'd asked. "You have to be my guinea pig, that's part of the deal." And Myrna had said a Brandy Alexander, thinking of *Days of Wine and Roses*, that movie she'd seen years ago with Jack Lemmon and Lee Remick as desperate, brutal alcoholics. They started out on Brandy Alexanders and that had always given the drink an extra little kick as far as Myrna was concerned, a special aura of power. Still did, even after she'd drunk her way through Gail's whole curriculum. Sidecars and Golden Cadillacs, Rusty Nails, Velvet Hammers.

When Gail moved into the apartment across from hers in the old building on Sydenham Street, Myrna was pregnant with Andrea, and Clarke was just walking. She had him in his stroller that day, coming back from the doctor's, when Gail got out of the taxi herding two toddlers, who didn't look to be more than a year apart, and lugging a huge suitcase. Myrna held the door open for her.

"If you need help with the rest of your stuff," she said, "I'm right across from you, in 3B."

"This is it."

Myrna thought she meant she was all moved in. Later, when she started babysitting for Stephen and Andrew, she saw that Gail had meant it, literally. By then, there was a mattress for the boys to sleep on and a couple of orange crates for chairs, but that was all.

For a long time, Myrna's picture of Gail's past life, in Calgary, was as sparse as the furnishings of that apartment. Gail had asked her to babysit, abruptly, about a week after she'd moved in. They'd met in the laundry room one afternoon. At the time it seemed to Myrna that Gail would have asked anyone. Anyone who just happened to be there, putting in the fabric softener, with a kid whining at her ankles, when Gail came down with her load, the two boys tagging along behind.

"I'm thinking of taking a bartending course at the college. Wednesday's, from half past six to ten o'clock," she said. No "hello" or anything – just that. "Do you think you could watch the boys? I'd have them in bed."

"Well, I . . . sure, I don't mind . . . at least until the baby comes," Myrna said.

Gail shot her an appraising glance. "Oh, I'll be finished before you are. You've got at least ten weeks to go there." And she turned, pushed the boys ahead of her, and went back upstairs.

Myrna just stood there. Even now she doesn't know why she didn't follow her to the door, yelling after her, "Kiss my ass, lady! You can mind your own stinking kids."

". . . But do you think he'll be all right?" Gail's voice, determined as always, dogging them all for an answer.

"I do, Gail. I think he'll be all right. I think what he's doing is very healthy, actually."

Selena. How can she be so sure? Especially when she can see that it's really bothering Gail.

"I don't know. I just think he should be over it by now. If I'd done the right thing, he'd be over it by now." Gail's voice has that wavery undercurrent in it again. It gives Myrna the shivers, the way it seems to carry her – and all of them – along with it.

"Over what?" Selena's laugh cuts through to that dark, small place. Or so it seems to Myrna. "And how do you know it's something *you* can fix? Besides, you think there's a schedule, Gail? A nice neat chart in the sky for all of us to follow. Stephen's going by his time, now, not . . . "

"Like you are, I suppose you mean?" Gail grins slightly, grudgingly. This is old ground, some of it.

Selena grins, too. Tosses that hair back, so that it shines like a blue halo around her. "Yeah, Gail, like me. Is that so terrible?"

Suzi Sims, once. Selena Bluestone, now. Suzi Sims, visited in a dream by a woman dressed entirely in blue. A woman who told her she must leave Greg and the boys, eat only white or blue foods, dress entirely in blue and change her name.

Selena Bluestone (she woke up, she claims, repeating this name) left that morning, with a toothbrush and the clothes on her back. Left Greg, the house, the boys – everything. Disappeared for ten days, till the next G5 gathering when she showed up (as they knew she would) with a veal and mushroom casserole. She'd shaved all her hair off, wrapped her head in a long, blue turban.

"To keep it together," she said. "Everything keeps spilling out."

Later, drunk, she stripped off her clothes and ran out into the snow in Nina's backyard. At first the rest of them stood on the deck, shivering like fools, helpless.

We've gone too far, Myrna kept thinking. *We've gone too far, this time.* Next door, the back porch light snapped on. Then, abruptly, off. *Now we've done it.*

It was Nina who stripped first, though. Then Myrna. Running into the snow.

"Gail? C'mon now. We can't carry on if we don't all make angels."

Nina. Did she really say that? Myrna hears herself laughing, falling back into the snow, the snow biting her skin raw. Did she really say that? Making it come out like a proverb or something. We can't carry on if we don't all make angels. You can't make an omelette if you don't break some eggs. Logical and necessary and easy and absurd. Like that.

The four of them, later, crowded into Nina's huge shower, screaming "My Blue Heaven" at the top of their lungs.

Selena is one of the country's most successful glass-blowers now, though at one time she wouldn't have known a piece of blown glass from a fifty-five-cent tumbler. Established artists, collectors, gallery curators are amazed at her technical sophistication, the lightness and balance of her pieces, their delicate, almost incandescent colour. And Selena herself is as calm, as serene as her name and her chosen colour imply.

There are flaws, of course. She "relates only to women now," as she puts it, but as far as Myrna can tell, the women she chooses are much like Greg and her sons. Blonde, athletic, humourless people who never ask questions and take up a lot of space in a room. They make Myrna's head ache and she is secretly glad that Selena, at present, is "completely off sex."

"Or between sexes," Nina says, laughing. "With Selena, who knows?"

You always have a choice, Myrna. You just may not want to make it.

You think there's a schedule, Gail?

Selena. The way she can say things like that.

When Myrna looks out now, the tow truck's half full of snow. It's been coming down for hours looks like; the big, silent kind that makes her feel as if she's been set adrift, she and the others, in this bright, warm room.

A night like this, driving that road from the airport, a little tired perhaps, you could easily miss the turn. It would be almost like sailing, she thinks, plunging into that field, the snow and the night flying like water around you.

And then sitting there, stopped, wide awake. Not knowing what to do, the cold starting to bite through your coat, wondering where your snowboots are.

Someone coming up with a flashlight, rapping on the window. "You all right, lady? Want me to call for a truck? I've got a CB."

It could be anybody who came like that, saying they wanted to help.

It used to scare her, sometimes, driving, especially at night when the kids were small. All those other cars whizzing around them, pulling out to pass after just the most casual glance in the rear mirror, everyone locked into their destinations, secret, secretive, the kids in the back seat impossibly fragile. You never knew, really, what anyone was going to do next, whether they were paying attention, whether they cared. And yet, if anything happened, these were the same people you'd have to count on to help you, you'd never know for sure, it could be anybody.

"And you're going to, really?" Nina cries, slobbering coffee down the front of her shirt in response to Selena's announcement. Gail is laughing wildly, pounding the table. They're all pretty drunk now. The last few Brandy Alexanders have been increasingly less precise. Selena has switched to beer.

"I don't know, I just don't know," she's screaming, laughing, tearing at her hair in mock anguish until it's standing up around her head, blue and electric. "It's just that he's so persistent!"

"You mean you're taking this seriously?" Gail looks up at her, sharply now. "God, Selena, he's twenty-fucking-five. You've got a kid that age." She shakes her head, but then she looks over at Myrna and gives her that quick, pinched smirk. The smirk, Myrna thinks, that parents exchange sometimes when the kid's done something really bad and they should be very angry, but it's funny, too, adorable at the same time.

"Well, I think it's very romantic. Two dozen roses, after all," Nina teases. "Were they blue?"

"As a matter of fact, they were."

"Selena! I do believe you're blushing!"

They're all pounding the table now, shrieking with laughter. Four sixteen-year-olds, drunk on Daddy's rye.

"You won't go back to being Suzi, though, will you?" Gail asks suddenly. "That would be taking it too far."

"Of course not," Selena smooths her hair down, smiling.

"But, seriously, what do you think?" She holds her hands out, palms up, across the table, grinning. "My life is in your hands."

And she means it, Myrna realizes. *Though she'll do whatever the hell she wants and let us know it, too, always the one with the advice and the judgements, because we can't keep up with her. That's only a part of it. This is another. She means it, her life is in our hands.*

The lights go out in the house next door and Myrna imagines how they must look to the travel agent and her tow truck driver. All lit up like this, the stereo blaring so loud they can probably hear it. Four middle-aged women sitting around a table full of dirty dishes in a kitchen that looks like it's been through a war, getting drunker than hell. She looks at Selena, with her bangles and her blue hair, at Gail in her old jeans with that T-shirt that says I'D RATHER BE PISSED OFF THAN ON, and she bursts out laughing, takes Selena's hands in her own.

Just as Nina giggles and says, "Go for it, Sel. I'm dying to hear what happens next." Making it all seem logical and necessary and easy and absurd, the way only Nina could make it.

Look at her now. The soft green of her shirt in the candlelight, her skin, the silk scarf flashing like those surprising glints you get in the plumage of some dark-feathered bird. Nina. Plump and complacent, smooth, like a dark and secretly exotic bird.

Easy to be Nina. Easy to see things the way she does. Daughter of a local businessman and the wife of Dr. Paul

Sorenson, more money than the rest of them will ever see in their whole lives.

Paul Sorenson is the obstetrician who delivered Brian. He was, in fact, in the very act of delivering Brian when his own daughter, Kelly, was born in the back seat of a careening taxi, on the way to the hospital.

"The shoemaker's wife goes shoeless," Nina always says, laughing, when she tells this story, "and the obstetrician's wife gets a nineteen-year-old speed-freak, just putting in a few hours for a friend. God, I thought for sure he was going to plough us into a telephone pole. I kept telling him to stop and radio for an ambulance and he kept saying, 'But what if it comes in the back seat. Oh, Frank is gonna kill me. He just had it cleaned.' Drivin' just as fast as he could."

She makes it sound like something out of some movie, absolutely improbable, like the chase scene that Myrna's kids love so much in *Beverly Hills Cop*. She never admits to being scared.

"But I really wasn't," she always says, matter-of-factly. "It was all so freaky, I figured it had to be meant. You know, destiny."

But that just means anything could have happened, Myrna thinks. *Anything.*

". . . And look at Kelly now," Nina always goes on, as if this were all obvious and necessary. The fact that her ten-year-old daughter is a speed swimmer, already expected to have a good chance at the Silver at the 1996 Olympics.

Though she could just as easily have ended up drooling in an institution somewhere, brain-damaged, the taxi crumbled into a stop sign, people coming up to the window, staring. It could have happened that way, too. What if, Nina. What if?

Myrna watches Nina take the last piece of cheesecake, licking the whipped cream off her fingers, calmly, dreamily. Her face has its familiar expression, the one that seems to Myrna to be sort of rapt and determined at the same time. The first time Myrna saw it was the day Nina came into her hospital room, two days after Brian was born.

"I told my husband he had to tell me whose baby it was," she'd said. "To hell with confidentiality. I'm Nina Sorenson and we were meant to be friends."

Meant to be. Destiny. Words like that. Words Myrna gets embarrassed by, even inside her own head. And Gail wouldn't say it if her life depended on it.

Beside her, Myrna catches Gail sneaking a look at her watch. Then she lights another cigarette, leans back in her chair, arms folded across her chest. Stephen again. Myrna can almost see him sitting there, right now, in Gail's apartment, in the steady blue light of the TV. She can even see Ward and June and Wally and the Beav, in black and white, just like they were when she and her brother Ross used to watch them, sitting on that green couch in the rec room back home with a plate of cookies and two glasses of chocolate milk on the coffee table in front of them. People you always thought you knew, somehow, like members of your own family.

Ross even believed that they went on living, inside the TV, after the program was over. "Their inside life," he used to call it. "They're going back to their inside life," he'd say every week when the credits rolled. And Myrna almost believes it now, in a way she never did then. It's what comes to her mind, at any rate, when she thinks of Stephen, when she sees him, leaning forward into the heart of that family, as if into an intimate conversation.

The first few times Myrna went to babysit for Gail, she'd be in her hallway, with her coat on, waiting, the kids already in bed. Sometimes she said "Hi" as she went out the door, sometimes she just pushed past her, as if Myrna's arrival were an interference in her plans. She never said "Thank you" when she got home, never asked if the kids had been okay. Though they always were. Myrna kept both doors open so that she could go from her apartment to Gail's, listening. Whenever she stuck her head into the boy's bedroom all she saw were two little bumps on the mattress. Maybe because the room was bare, the mattress looked tiny, adrift. Even the boys' breathing was cautious and small.

One night, she got there early and when no one answered her knock, let herself in. She could hear water splashing, Gail's voice in the bathroom.

"Hello," she called, "it's just me." But almost as she spoke, Gail appeared in the hallway, her fists clenched.

"Get the fuck out of . . . oh, it's you," she said, before Myrna could take this in. "I'll be right there."

She turned, but as she did so, Stephen escaped from the bathroom, giggling, stark naked as he tore towards Myrna, who opened her arms, instinctively, to scoop him up.

"Stephen, get back here!"

But Myrna caught him first, swung him up, laughing, though even as she did so she could feel the child stiffen.

That's when she saw the ring of small, round, white welts, like pockmarks on his buttock, just as Gail reached for him. Their eyes met.

"His father used to do that with a cigarette," Gail said, "whenever he peed himself."

She held her right hand, back out, in front of Myrna's face. The raised white scar ripped across it from the base of her thumb to the base of her ring finger.

"And he closed the door on my hand, the first time I tried to get away. So now you know." She took Stephen from Myrna's arms, set him on the floor and turned away.

"I'm not goin' tonight," she said, over her shoulder. "You don't need to stay." She gave Stephen a shove towards the bedroom.

It was their backs Myrna saw. Gail's, and then Stephen's, just ahead of her. Their skinny necks and shoulders, bone-thin, pinched to identical angles of guilt and defeat.

That's when she reached out and took Gail in her arms, gave her a quick hug. "Nonsense. Get your coat on," she said.

"That's when you saved my life," Gail told her, years later.

And Myrna, now, remembers the feel of her body, rigid and small, like Stephen's, exactly like Stephen's had felt a few minutes earlier. Remembers it so clearly, in fact, that she's not surprised at all when Gail suddenly leans forward, cradles her head in her arms on the table and begins to sob. Hesitantly, at first, as if the sobs themselves are embarrassed to be heard, and then harder, urgent, so that for a split second Myrna thinks of Gail earlier in the evening, slamming those bottles onto the counter.

For a moment, no one moves. And then, it seems to Myrna they all move at once, perfectly, in unison. And as she turns towards Gail, she sees the four of them there, reflected in the glass beside her. Sees Selena, already on her feet, her chair thrown over, her hands coming down gently on Gail's hair. And Nina, right behind her, with a box of Kleenex in her hand. She sees how Selena's hair lights up the room the way the snow lights up the night outside. She sees the small of Gail's back and her thin, thin shoulders. Sees her own face, flushed and oddly beautiful as she leans down towards Gail's sobs and whatever country they will open for her now. And she sees how the light shines out from them all – into the dark yard, the street, the tow truck filling up with snow.

THE SCUBA DIVER
IN REPOSE

Jimmie had been dead about six months when I ripped up all the photos. I came home late from work and the apartment was dark and stinking and filthy and there was nothing to eat in the fridge, and I think that's when it really hit me. He wasn't coming back, ever.

"You bastard! You goddamn fucking bastard!" It was like the words took me over and there was this new place inside my chest that got bigger and hotter the more I yelled.

I started with the photographs on the bookcase, tearing them out of their frames and ripping them into little pieces. None of this Hollywood bullshit where you see some woman cut the guy out of the picture and leave herself, smiling, intact. To hell with that.

Then the albums. And all the stuff in the spare bedroom. All my neat little files, contact sheets, negs, everything. There was a roll of film still in my Nikon, stuff I'd been taking at the time. I didn't want to know. I ripped it out and threw the camera against the wall. I wanted to obliterate everything, all the evidence. I wanted it to look like what it felt.

Afterwards I lay on the bed, screaming and crying. I could hear someone knocking softly on the apartment door. Mrs. Harmen from upstairs wanting to know if I was all right. I shoved my face into the pillow and let her knock. After a while she went away.

I lay on the bed for a long time. The space inside my chest cooled and contracted, a hard lump the size of my fist. Around midnight, I got up, shoved everything into a garbage bag and took it down to the trash bin in the basement. I could hear Mrs. Harmen's door open sneakily when I came back upstairs, but I ignored it, locked the door and went to bed.

The next day I shovelled out the apartment, washed the walls and the curtains, windows, floors, shampooed the rug, the whole bit. I'd already given most of Jimmie's stuff to his parents or to Kyle, but now I took his jean jacket that I still wore sometimes, along with a couple of shirts I found in the back of the closet down to the Goodwill. And his scuba-diving equipment. The lady there wasn't so sure about the scuba-diving equipment. They'd never sold it before and it was expensive, wasn't it, but I said take it, it doesn't matter and it didn't.

On the way home I bought flowers and a bottle of wine, a big steak, fresh vegetables, some gourmet coffee. The apartment looked warm and bright, the way it used to. I smoked a joint, cooked myself a great dinner, drank some wine, smoked another joint with my coffee. I played all my Judy Collins records. Jimmie hated Judy Collins. He said she couldn't sing worth shit.

I was feeling pretty good. I almost considered inviting Mrs. Harmen down to finish off the bottle. I figured this was what people who were into therapy meant by getting in touch with their anger. Discharging.

All that bullshit.

Sure, I felt great for a while. Several weeks, in fact. But Jimmie was still dead. I couldn't change that, no matter how good I felt at the moment.

When my sister Lee and I were little, I was the "easy-going" one, she was "high-strung." Later it was "laid-back" and "control-freak," but you get the picture. I'm supposed to pull through because I'm placid, flexible.

What I am, really, is drifting. Not on keel. Up shit's creek without a paddle.

After I finished high school I had no idea what I wanted to be, but I thought I'd like to travel in Europe for a while. My French teacher, M. Poulin, got me a job as an au pair with a cousin outside of Nice and I stayed for a year. They sent me on to relatives in Switzerland and then I just went from job to job until I came home.

It seemed like I'd never been away. I still didn't know what I wanted to do, so I got a job as a teller at Canada Trust.

Lee had given me a second-hand Canon and a bag of film as a going-away present. ("I know you'll never write," she'd said, "so send me pictures.") When I got back, she laid them all out for me, all the stuff I'd sent her. Even I could see that I got better as I went along, especially with people, the Poulin kids in particular.

"You're good," Lee kept saying. "Why don't you take some lessons? You know, get some fine points on technique or whatever."

Lee knew nothing about photography, but she's the type that figures you should take a course in something if you want to learn it. Sometimes she's right. I did take a few courses and I learned a fair amount, especially about developing. Pretty soon I was taking pictures whenever I had time, living in a dump and spending everything I could on equipment and film.

I loved looking at other people's photographs. Everything and anything. Steiglitz, Arbus, Strand, Bourke-White. I knew all the big names, but I loved people's family snapshots, too, slides of my uncle's umpteenth trip to Key West. I wanted to see it all.

Things had been going along like this for about five years when I met Jimmie. He moved into another apartment in my building, one that was even more of a rat hole than my place. It was also cheaper, which, I found out later, was why he took it. I don't think I really noticed him at first, except in the hall, a tall, scruffy-looking guy who always seemed to be in a hurry. I can't even remember how we started talking or how it was that he ended up in my apartment one Saturday, drinking beer. Of course, he saw the photographs. They were everywhere.

"These are great!" he kept saying, waving his arms around, sloshing beer all over. "I didn't know you were a photographer. Why did you say you were a teller?"

"Because that's what I do, really. This is just a hobby."

"No," Jimmie said then, very seriously, "you're a teller 'cause you need the money, right? But these photographs are your real work. This is what you love."

Real work. Love. That was the way he described himself.

"I'll do anything legal for money," he'd say. "Construction, taxi, assembly line, you name it. But for love, for my real work, I'm a scuba diver."

He'd been all over the Caribbean – the Bahamas, the Caymens – he'd been to Cuba, but the thing about Jimmie was that he was just as happy diving at Tobermory or puddling around in one of the little lakes near here. He just liked being down there, looking.

"You have to learn how to use your eyes all over again," he said. "It's a whole new world. That's what I like about it."

Maybe it was that day – or soon after – that I showed him a book of photographs by Jacques-Henri Lartigue. He loved them, especially the ones Lartigue took when he was really young, eleven or so. There was one in particular – "At the Races, Auteuil, 1910" – in which, in a huge crowd of people, Lartigue has caught two men eyeing a beautiful woman. It's just a quick glance, you understand, you know they're going to look away in a second, they're too much gentlemen to stare. Jimmie loved that. He said to get a shot like that you would have to be able to look at the world the way a kid does – as if it were all just happening for the first time.

He was probably right. Jimmie was always going on about how we learn not to look at things as we grow up. He used to say that the only astronaut he respected was Ed White, the guy who freaked out on his space walk and became so euphoric about it all that he refused to get back into the capsule. When he did get back, he said it was the saddest moment of his life. As far as Jimmie was concerned, White was the only one of them who really saw where he was and what he was doing. The others could have been in a shopping mall, he said, for all they let on.

" 'One giant step for mankind,' " he'd say. "Jesus, it sounds like a campaign speech. What does that tell you about what the guy felt?"

Whenever I was with Jimmie – and we could be talking or making love or even cleaning up the apartment – I knew, really knew, what I was doing. I don't know how else to say it. Sometimes I even said to myself, hey, this is it, I'm actually living my life, I'm in charge, but mostly I didn't even need to. Mostly I was just paying attention for the first time in my life.

And it was this – Jimmie's *presence*, I guess you'd call it – that I *decided*, yes decided, that I wanted to photograph. It took me ages and hundreds of tries, but I finally got it.

I could tell even as it was coming up in the tray that I had it. It was one of those things, I just knew, though it didn't look like him at all. Jimmie was big, almost six foot three inches and broad shouldered, but in this photo he looked shorter, more my height, and thin. He was leaning on the windowsill of our apartment (the one I'm in now, we'd just moved to it then), looking down on something in the street. I'd shot him from behind and to the side, so that you saw his profile, partly, and a scraggly halo of hair, his shoulders hunched as he leaned forward, his arms hanging over the sill. There was a stillness to it all that was more like movement, if you know what I mean. I don't think he knew I was taking the picture at the time, but that doesn't matter because whatever he was looking at was what mattered to him, *all* that mattered to him right then, and somehow I'd managed to get that in the picture.

It got me thinking. I had this idea for trying to shoot other people like this, people I thought I knew pretty well – my parents, Lee and her kids, Jimmie's son Kyle who spent most of his holidays with us, a couple of the women at work. I didn't know exactly what I was after. To say "something essential, something true about each person" seemed too much. I just knew I'd recognize it.

The project took two years. It was the first time in my life I'd ever even thought of anything as a project like that, as if I *meant* to do it. It was also the best stuff I'd done, ever.

It was also a surprise, every time, what came up. And I began to see that very often people were most themselves when they didn't look it, when they were unrecognizable in all the usual ways.

Lee, for example. I worked like hell on hers, it had to be just right. But in the end the one I liked best was an old snapshot I'd taken with the Canon just after I got back from Europe. Lee was pregnant with Allison then. It was July and about eighty-five in the shade, for weeks. In the picture, Lee's belly is enormous and she's sprawled in a kid's inflatable wading pool in their backyard, her legs out over the sides, like a beached whale. She's got her head back against the top ring of the pool and she's drinking a beer while her son Danny – who was three at the time – is spraying her belly with the hose.

Describing it like that makes it sound merely silly, especially if you know Lee. But there's something serious about it, too, about the way Lee manages to look so calm, so, so *competent*, even like that. The way she manages, no matter what. Unlike me.

Anyway, the Elsa Fleming Gallery, a small place connected to the university, accepted the prints for a show they were doing on local artists. I couldn't believe it, anymore than I could believe I'd actually entered them in the first place. But there they were: "The Scuba Diver in Repose, and Friends. Gillian Stewart, 1981-84."

Jimmie was beside himself with excitement. He loved the photographs, the idea behind them, the local prestige of my being accepted at the gallery. He made sure everyone came – his parents, Kyle, Ruth (his ex, who was still a good friend, I like her, too), the guys he was working with, people he met on the street. He bought champagne and roses and, being Jimmie, managed to do it all without showing off. He was just Jimmie, genuinely pleased for me, but celebrating his pleasure for himself.

Not everyone got as excited as he did or even as pleased. Some, like Lee, were just sort of embarrassed, but one of the women from work, Helen, was actually angry. My parents didn't even recognize themselves. I began to think that maybe I'd made a big mistake, gone too far or something, exposed people, people I loved to, to . . . I didn't know what.

"But that's why it's so great, Jill," Jimmie said after everyone had left.

He walked around the room again, as he had a dozen times, pausing before each photograph. At his own, he turned back towards me.

"You've shown up all our secret and difficult and hard-to-get-at places. And then," he came towards me, talking excitedly, waving his arms the way he did, until you thought they might come loose, "and then – and this is the really exciting part – you've put us all together so that we have to see that each of us is like that. As different in ourselves as we are from each other." He nodded to the walls again. "And that's hard to take."

I was embarrassed now. I'd never thought of it that way, really. "Don't you think you're making too much of this?"

He looked at me, the way he did sometimes, as if he were seeing me for the first time. "But you did shoot all those pictures, Jill, and you did put them together this way." He toasted them with the last of his champagne. "You must have known some of it at least, don't you think?"

A caretaker came to the door and began sweeping impatiently. Jimmie took the hint, put his glass down and moved off to find his coat.

Outside it was raining and we ran for a cab, drunker than we'd thought. There was something else I wanted to ask him, but it got all blurry out there in the rain, and anyway I didn't know how. Three months later, he was dead.

Chorio carcinoma. There might have been a time when Jimmie and I would have taken a phrase like that and played with it. Jimmie might have said it sounded like something from opera, I might have argued for an Italian film star. But that day it was impossible to say, it meant so many things.

Just after my show, we'd gone to the Bahamas for two weeks, but near the end of it Jimmie started feeling really tired. Too much diving, he said, but when we got home it was worse, some kind of bug obviously, he was vomiting all the time. Then he got jaundiced and I thought *hepatitis,* though I wasn't sure how you got that. By the time he went to the doctor, I could see that I didn't know much about anything in there, inside you, what went on.

Blood tests, first of all. Liver scan. Ultrasound. Biopsy, chest x-ray, brain scan.

Liver.

Jimmie was sitting up in bed feeling not too bad and I was in the chair beside him when Dr. Jamieson came in, sat down in the chair on the other side of the bed.

"Jimmie, we have the results of the biopsy."

"And?"

"Well, as we suspected, there is definitely cancer in the liver, though it originated somewhere else certainly. We're thinking that it probably originated in the testicle."

Seeding. They call it seeding. The cells are seeded into the bloodstream, picked up in another organ. Metastases. Glandular cells from the testicle. Liver. Chorio carcinoma.

"So what does that mean, exactly?"

Dr. Jamieson was quiet for a minute. I mean, he made the pause part of what he was saying. Then he looked straight at Jimmie.

"When you've got cancer in the liver," he said, "there's not a lot we can do. *For the cancer.*"

I heard it like that, emphasized, as if they wanted to care for it the way you care for a baby.

"And for me?" Jimmie asked. "What can you do for me?"

"We'll do our best to keep you comfortable, Jim."

"You're saying that I'm going to die." Not even a question. He didn't even have to ask.

"Yes."

Up until this point, Jimmie had been holding my hand. Now he let go. For a long time, this was one of the things I went over and over. Now, sometimes, I begin to understand. What he started on that day, he started on alone.

"So, how long have I got?"

"Again, Jim, it varies with the individual. Some people in this situation could be dead in a week, some will go on living for several months."

"But what you're saying is that I'll be dead in a few months."

Dr. Jamieson was quiet again. He shifted in his chair, leaned forward.

"Yes," he said. "Yes."

Outside the window it was just a regular day, around rush hour. I watched the people getting on and off the buses that pulled up in front of the hospital. I could hear horns and kids laughing and pigeons cooing on a window ledge nearby, all of it louder than Dr. Jamieson's and Jimmie's voices which went on behind me.

I turned back to them.

"What you need to complete," Dr. Jamieson was saying, "and I mean practical stuff, financial and all, as well as your son and your parents and Jill." He looked at me for a moment. Jimmie did, too. "What you need to complete before you die."

I got panicky then. But not about his dying. Crazy stuff, like how I was going to schedule time at the hospital and still keep my job. How many people we could put up in the apartment. There'd be Jimmie's brother Stan, and Ruth and Kyle. I even started planning meals, every detail, I wanted to get a grip on everything. At the same time I felt overwhelmed. Pissed off, too, like when you're getting ready for house guests you're not quite sure you should have invited.

As it turned out, things didn't go at all the way I thought they would. And yet it was all familiar, somehow, even at the time.

"It's what I've never seen before that I recognize." Diane Arbus says that, in the preface to one of her collections.

And Jimmie's dying was just like that.

He wanted to die at home, not in the hospital, so once that was clear, everything else fell into place.

It was obvious immediately that our apartment wouldn't do. The stairs for one thing. The size of the bedroom. So Jimmie would go to his parents', to Marge and Keith's place, a few miles out of town. I would stay there. ("As much as you want," Marge said, as if this were something you decided about.)

This left our apartment (*my* apartment, really. Already.) free for people from out of town. Stan, Jimmie's brother, whenever he came from Victoria. Ruth and Kyle.

As it turned out, Ruth took a leave of absence and pulled Kyle out of school. Just like that. She said it was too important to Kyle to do anything else. They stayed in my apartment the whole time. The whole nine weeks.

I thought it was great, really, her doing that. For Kyle, for herself. Ruth was a lot like Lee, capable and intelligent, sure of herself. She kept pretty much out of the way, taking care of the practical stuff. Finances, lawyers, funeral arrangements. She did all that, I'm sure, knowing Ruth, so I could have more time with Jimmie. And I did, I was always there.

But what I felt was displaced. It didn't have anything to do with Ruth, or even with the apartment. It was just how I felt. Like I was one of those guests at some big do who isn't really a central figure, someone you don't care about, whether they're in the frame or not.

Part of it was that I'd never really seen Jimmie in his life before, his whole life, I mean, all its webs and connections. Mostly, before, there'd just been him and me, Kyle during the holidays, his parents for a meal sometimes, each of them separate, separable.

Now, everyone kept crowding in. Marge was always in the kitchen, never far from the door to his room. She kept making his favourite dishes, though he couldn't keep anything down. She kept saying things like, "You'll need your strength, son."

"For what?" he screamed at her once. I was in the doorway, behind her, she'd just brought in this soup she'd spent hours on, we'd had to go to six stores just to find the ingredients. And he grabbed it out of her hand and threw it at the wall. Like a kid would. I remember thinking that. Like a kid would, having a temper tantrum. Mad at his mother.

"What am I keeping up my fucking strength for, woman, answer me that." Woman. He called her "woman." Like it was the worst insult he could think of. And then he just grabbed her around the hips, she was standing by his bed, she had on a pink apron, I remember, with cornflowers embroidered on it. He grabbed her around the hips and buried his face in her belly and all I could see were his shoulders shaking and her hands stroking his hair.

I went out then, into the garden, and threw up behind the garage. It was like the time I nearly got hit by a car, coming home from school on my bike when I was a kid, my knees felt all watery, I remember, standing by the curb and throwing up, I couldn't stop retching. And both times, the feeling was the same, too, that feeling that comes all over you when you realize there really isn't anyone there to protect you from anything, anymore.

And Kyle. He was eleven then, small and dark, like Ruth, with the same thick, curly hair. He spent hours playing Scrabble with Jimmie or getting him to teach him how to play the guitar, though Jimmie was no hell himself, just a few songs. Towards the end, they'd read comics together, Kyle curled up on the bed beside Jimmie, even when he fell asleep. He looked so much like Ruth, his head there on the pillow beside Jimmie's. Sometimes I thought . . .

I only her heard crying once, Ruth. Both of them, actually, crying. The door was closed, as it seldom was and Marge took me, firmly, away, out to the garden where the pink was just starting to show at the tips of the peony buds.

Details like that. They filled up everywhere. The peony buds, or coming to the door one day to see Keith, Jimmie's dad, leaning over the bed, his head almost on Jimmie's chest and Jimmie's arm, long, white, impossibly thin against the dark of his jacket. The thick, cramped sound of male sobs as I turned away.

Stan. He got in one night around midnight, about a week before Jimmie died. He'd been calling almost every day before that with advice about diets, vitamins. Crazy stuff – wheat-grass enemas, herbal teas.

That night he stood in the door of Jimmie's room and wouldn't even speak, just stood there, rigid. And after that he spent most of his time on the back steps, chain-smoking and staring, his shoulders thin, stark with anger, you could feel it all around him.

You could feel all of us, everywhere, all the time.

We'd put Jimmie in the big room at the back of the house, off the kitchen. A sun room, really, though Marge used it as a sewing room. Warm and bright, there were windows all around, looking over the garden which was just coming out, it was mid-April. Masses of scillae and snowdrops at first, crocuses, daffodils and forget-me-nots, bleeding heart, peonies near the end. Marge kept saying it was the best her garden had ever been. She said it every morning, in fact, the way gardeners do, so that you knew her pleasure wasn't just for Jimmie's sake, it was also for her own.

I spent hours out there, in the garden, taking pictures.

"It takes her mind off things," Keith said once to a neighbour, nodding in my direction, as if I couldn't hear. He was a big-boned, practical man, a retired cop, who kept himself busy fixing stuff around the house the whole time.

Actually, I was trying to get my mind *on* things, on Jimmie. I was trying to focus. But everything kept shifting, fading away.

No, I mean Jimmie. Jimmie kept shifting and fading, faster than I could keep up. Every time I came in from the garden he was thinner; the bones of his face, which had always seemed sort of loose and scraggy to me, became firmer, almost delicate. He'd had his hair cut short before he left the hospital and now it started to grey almost overnight. Maybe that was it. Or the way his mother kept him clean shaven.

Mostly he was alert, though he tired easily. They'd had to operate to clear his liver and he had a bag we had to clean three or four times a day, clamping off the tube that ran from the incision under his rib cage and emptying the dark, grainy bile.

He said that dying was a lot like being underwater – drifting, watching everything drift. He said it was like learning to breathe the first time you dived, how you had to trust the equipment, not be afraid of being underwater. That way you could pay attention to everything around you, he said. He said the floaty feeling was the same, too, he could feel parts of himself sort of going away, feel himself letting go of them. He said he had to pay attention, to say goodbye to the use of his legs, his stomach, whole parts of his brain, memories. He kept listing stuff like that, trying to get me to understand. See what it was like.

And I tried, I really did. But he was dying and I wasn't. I saw his pain, I worried about making him comfortable, about changing his bag, about medications, smells. I saw what the living see, I guess, as much as I could stand, and it was too much. I wanted it over.

And then it was. June 15, 1984. Jimmie and I had been alone most of the afternoon. It was a beautiful day and Marge and Keith had gone for a drive. Kyle came in for a while, fooling around with Jimmie's guitar.

"You're getting pretty good, Kyle," Jimmie told him. "A lot better than I ever was."

"Dad?"

"Yes."

"Can I have it then, the guitar, when you . . . " He stopped.

Jimmie was quiet for a while. It was part of his answer, I think now. I think he wanted us to hear it, that silence where we're afraid to say what we have to.

"Yes, Kyle," he said finally. "You can have it. When I die."

He gave him a big hug and then Ruth came and I saw them to the door and when I came back Jimmie was asleep. I sat there for maybe an hour, maybe less, listening to his breathing, watching that little flutter, like a shadow, in the hollow of his throat. His arms lay at his sides, outside the sheet. His hands were enormous, too big for him, like the paws on a pup you know has a lot of growing to do. I was just wondering about whether or not to start supper when he gave these three big – sort of sighs, I guess.

And stopped. That was it. I waited, holding my breath, but there wasn't anymore. And then Marge and Keith came in and everyone, everything else started moving again. Except for Jimmie. And for me. I've been holding my breath, one way or another it seems, for a long, long time.

Whenever he could, Jimmie was off diving somewhere and when I could get time off work, I went with him, though I never wanted to try it myself, I was too busy on land, taking pictures. We'd saved for that trip to the Bahamas for ages. It was my first time there and I don't think I slept at all the first week, there was so much I wanted to shoot. The light and the colour. I'd never done much colour stuff before and now I had to learn how to see it, really see it, instead of just trying to see everything in shades of grey.

On a good day I like to remember us like that, Jimmie and me. I like to see myself on the beach, learning to see colour in that high, harsh light, the blue ocean and Jimmie out there somewhere, under it, invisible but safe. Looking at fish he'd try to describe to me later, his hands swimming and flopping in the pale grey light of our bedroom. On a good day I can see that maybe we're still like that somehow, each of us moving deeper into whatever world we've found, still attached.

On a good day, that is, and for a few minutes, no more. A glimpse, from the corner of my eye.

Last Monday was my birthday. I knew they'd have a cake for me at work and flowers probably, cards. So I called in sick, hating myself for doing it, but knowing I couldn't face that. I can't take people's good wishes, their kindness anymore. I am like those kids I've read about in magazines, kids whose skin is so sensitive the slightest touch leaves a bruise.

It's not the day-to-day, you understand. I do fine at work with the customers, maintain the coffee-break chatter. But I don't go out with the others after work anymore. I hardly ever see Marge and Keith and even when I call, I have trouble getting my voice to work, as if I had a bad throat. Kyle wrote months ago – he's taller than Ruth now – and I haven't answered. What does it matter, really? I was only in his life such a short time anyway. In his past. I don't see how I can be anywhere else anymore.

After I ripped up the photographs I thought it was going to be different. Better. Clearer, maybe. I even started dating this guy, Derek Anderson, but I had to stop. I couldn't keep up my end of things, supporting his liking me, I couldn't. So mostly things just go on and I spent my birthday in bed. The only person I didn't manage to avoid was Tina.

Tina Pringle. She moved in a few months ago. Jimmie would have noticed how much she looks like her name sounds. Sort of sprightly and perky and wiry. She has one of those high-boned little faces where the skin's so fine it seems to register everything, double-quick, everything she feels, everything she says. From the beginning I could read her eagerness, her wanting to be friends, and I just went along with it and never let on. Not about Jimmie, not about anything.

She didn't even know it was my birthday when she caught me in hall in my bathrobe. I'd gone down for the mail and she was just getting off work.

"You sick?" she asked.

I nodded.

"You look awful. Why don't you go back to bed and I'll bring you down some soup or something." She was already sort of herding me back upstairs, so I just let her.

She came back down with some soup, some cheese and crackers, slices of fruit. She opened the curtains and fluffed up my pillows, pretending not to notice that the place was a pigsty.

She pulled up a chair beside my bed, took a piece of cheese and said, "You never told me you were a photographer." Just like that.

"That's because I'm not." For a minute, I wanted to add "anymore" but I couldn't seem to manage it. Though

I should have known. Tina works for the paper here. She'd been researching something else when she came across a piece about the show. And she wouldn't let me get away with anything.

"The article was so positive, Jill. Why don't you take pictures anymore?"

So I let her have it. Jimmie, the exhibition, the chorio carcinoma, the rampage, everything. I could feel the words spilling out from that same hot place inside my chest, getting bigger and hotter. But this time I was inside there, somehow, calling out.

Then I was crying and I couldn't stop. I could see Tina's face. It was all I could see and it seemed that everything was there. For a minute, everything sharpened up. She had a little splash of freckles around her left eye, sort of a half-moon as if someone had sprinkled cinnamon there to emphasize her cheekbones. I wanted to say something about it, but the tears took over and I let her hold me until they stopped. Then she tucked me into bed.

When I woke up, I saw she'd left my mail stacked on the night table. Cards, mostly. From Lee and my parents. The one from Kyle was handmade. It had a bird and two sheep and some big animal, I couldn't tell what, on the outside. Inside it said, "Hippo, birdie, two ewes. Ha, ha. Love, Kyle." There was nothing from Marge and Frank.

Until today, that is. I've made it to Friday, avoiding Tina all week, and I like to think I'm doing fine, thank you very much. I'm not even paying attention when I open their card. I don't even see – no, I pretend not to see –

what falls out onto the floor. I read Marge's note instead. "Happy Birthday, dear. We thought you might like to have this. Love, Marge and Frank."

I look down for it, then, and pick it up, turn it over.

He looks to be about five here. It's his birthday party and he's just about to blow out the candles, leaning forward, his face partially hidden by the other kids, partially blurred by his own movement, intent on *that*.

"It's what I've never seen before that I recognize."

Jimmie. Oh, Jimmie.

Jimmie, you were dying in that bright room and not one of us could stop you. Not with our soups or our crying, our goddamn wheat-grass enemas, our songs or anything. We couldn't. You weren't paying attention. To us. Anymore. You'd already moved on to check out something else, over there, you were already moving through it and it took every ounce of strength you had to see just exactly what it was. When you surfaced, it was only for a moment, that was all you had, after all, and it was up to us to be there, ready. To say what we had to say, to do it, alone, with you, for the last time.

That is what you gave us, what we saw, each of us, in our own way.

Kyle standing there with his fingers curled around the neck of your guitar.

The sunlight falling over my shoulder onto the white sheet, your hands there, huge and open.

Right now this snapshot is the only one I have in the world. I get some tape and stick it on the wall above the kitchen table.

The sound of someone banging on the door comes to me from a long way off.

Tina.

"I'm going for pizza. Wanna come?"

That crescent of freckles, those beautiful bones. Right now, I can see them perfectly. Maybe not from now on, but right now, I can see them, perfectly. It hurts my eyes. Just as I know it will hurt my hand a little, the first time I touch her. The first time I take that face in my hands to tilt it, just so, into the light.

Acknowledgements

An earlier version of "Chicken 'n' Ribs" appears in *event* (17,2) and in *The Journey Prize Anthology* (McClelland & Stewart Inc. 1989). "Heart of My Heart" has appeared in *Arc* (spring 1988) and in *Best Short Stories '88* (Oberon Press). "For Puzzled in Wisconsin" first appeared in a slightly altered version in *Quarry* (summer 1988). "Back Pain" appeared in *The Canadian Forum* (January 1990). "People You'd Trust Your Life To" will appear in the Spring 1990 fiction supplement in *Country Estate*.

In writing these stories I was particularly glad of information, editorial comment and especially steadfast interest and support from the following people: Blaine Allan, Donna Bennett, Russell Brown, David Helwig, Diane Schoemperlen, Carolyn Smart, Diana Wyatt and Dale Zieroth.

At least two of these stories were begun during a wonderful two-week retreat at the Saskatchewan Writers' Colony, St. Peter's Abbey, Muenster, Saskatchewan, in June of 1987. I was there as a guest of the Saskatchewan Writers' Guild and would like to thank the Guild for that opportunity.

I am also grateful to the financial support of the Ontario Arts Council and the Canada Council.

Bronwen Wallace
Kingston, Ontario
August 1989